NASH

Sheppard's Shadow Book 1

KATHI S. BARTON

This is a work of fiction. Names, characters, places, and incidents are products of the author's imagination or are used fictitiously and are not to be construed as real. Any resemblance to actual events, locations, organizations, or persons, living or dead, is entirely coincidental.

World Castle Publishing, LLC
Pensacola, Florida

Copyright © 2023 Kathi S. Barton
Paperback ISBN: 9798891261280
eBook ISBN: 9798891261297
First Edition World Castle Publishing, LLC, December 22, 2023
http://www.worldcastlepublishing.com

Licensing Notes

Cover: Cover Designs by Karen
https://www.cover-designs-by-karen.com
Editor: Karen Fuller

Chapter 1

Nash didn't bother buttoning his pants when he pulled them on. Leaning over, he reached for his shirt and didn't bother with trying to make it look presentable either as he pulled it up and over his head. Standing, he made his way to his shoes and sat down on the only clean surface in the room. Christ, had he had a look around before going to her bed, he might well have gone on home and jerked off.

"Hey, big boy. Why don't you come back to bed? I'll make it worth your while to be late to work." He didn't bother saying anything. His temper, always so close lately, had gotten him in trouble with more than one hooker of late. Not to mention his family. "Come on. We can make another go of it."

"No." Standing after pulling on his shoes, he reached for the cash he had in his pocket. Tossing another fifty on the top of her nasty dresser, he decided it was well past time for him to get out of here.

"You're not too terribly friendly, are you?" Again, he didn't answer. Sometimes, it was best to keep his mouth shut. Or so everyone in his family had been telling him lately. "Yeah, I can see you don't even think of me as a person. Don't bother coming back either."

"All right." As soon as he leaned over to pick up his coat, he felt something fly over his head. Looking at the naked woman in the bed, he glared at her. "You're getting emotional on me? That's why I go to your kind and not humans. Less said, no drama and certainly no feelings hurt because I want it done and over with."

"My kind? What the hell is that supposed to mean?" He told her shifter and hooker. "I'm not a hooker, you fuck. I'm a prostitute. Where do you get off calling me — get out of here before I call in Mason. He'll show you the difference between *my kind*."

He didn't have any idea what the fuck that was supposed to mean, but he did get the last of his things and left. Nash was more than happy that he paid at the beginning of his night rather than at the end. It tended to be cheaper, and he didn't have to linger around trying to figure out what she deemed to be a good price.

Once he was out on the street, he made his way to downtown. It was nearly six in the morning, so he didn't have to worry about too many people on the sidewalks. Even having someone touching him of late would send him into a rage that he couldn't imagine someone living through if he were to unleash it.

Going by his apartment, he showered and then put on a suit. Might as well get himself to work before anyone else. He wouldn't have to explain himself, nor would anyone bother him unless his door was open. Keeping it closed and locked had saved his family a lot of wars. All he'd been able to share with them was his anger and more anger.

Nearly turning around and going back home when he saw who was in his office; his mom stood up and told him to have a seat. He could tell that she was in as bad a mood as he was, so he didn't push her buttons by telling her that he didn't want to talk to her today. Or any day, for that matter.

"How many people do I have to pay off that you pissed off on the way in today, Nashville?" He just sat at his desk and looked at her. "In the event you didn't understand that. It was a question that I want an answer for. Who have you blistered with your temper this morning?"

"Since I know for a fact that you are aware of when the staff comes in, then I'm not going to answer that since it's just after seven. And unless you want to add yourself to that list you seem to be wanting to add to, then I want you to know that I'm in no mood to fool with anything you might have to say to me today." He knew, just as soon as the words slipped from his lips, that he'd pissed off the one person in the world that wouldn't have a bit of trouble taking him on. Verbally, of course, but there would be no fewer wounds than if it was one of his brothers. "What is it you want, Mother? I'm not in the mood for anything."

"No, everyone that is around you can see that. Feel it, too. You and your brothers have been peeling the skin off of every person who dares to come near you. Yesterday, I had to beg Archie's secretary not to quit. Then, this morning, I had to handle a very personal call about you. Did you really call someone a hooker?" He wasn't going to be embarrassed about his mom knowing about his sex life. If she didn't want to know, then she should keep her nose out of his business. "Well?"

"One, you knowing that I did that boggles my mind. Why would you even care that I'm fucking anyone, much less someone that I have to pay? Two. Where the hell do you get off coming in here and giving me grief because I got my rocks off?" When she stood up, so did he. He could see the anger in her eyes and hoped to Christ, she'd back off. "Go home, Mom. I've got a great deal of work—"

The hand to his face hurt. Not the pain of it, though, that did sting, but the fact that he'd driven his mother to slapping him. When the other side of his face exploded in pain, he took a step back from her.

His mother wasn't a typical mother. Beautiful, she was tall, nearly as tall as he was at six feet four inches and slight. But she was a shifter, the same as he was, and she could, if she wanted, release as much of her cat as she deemed necessary. It appeared that she thought this was one of those times to release a great deal of her.

"I don't know who you think you're talking to, but if you ever use that tone or language with me again, I will end you, Nashville Peterson Sheppard. I won't regret it nearly as much as you will when I stand over your bleeding throat and watch you die." His cat, usually right out there ready to do battle, curled back and away from his mother. "If you think that I'm the least bit warry of doing it, then you just try me."

Stretching his neck, it popped. When he bent his head to do the other side of his neck, he heard the distinguishable sound of claws unsheathing. Taking another step back from his mom, he looked at her claws. Even with the light shade of pink nail polish she had on them, he knew them to be lethal. And that she was finished with fucking with him.

"This is me talking to you in a low, somewhat calm voice. Gather up what you need from this office and go home. Don't you dare set foot across the threshold, or so help me, I will do as I said to you. You're not to be here, not even to call in, until I grant you access to this building. Do I make myself clear?" He said yes through clinched teeth. "This, whatever this is that you're doing or feeling, myself and the rest of the staff here have had enough."

When she turned on her heel, it was on the tip of his tongue to speak again. He knew as well as he was standing there that it would not end well for himself, but Nash couldn't stop himself. As his mother paused at the door, her claws still out where she could use them if necessary, she looked at him once again.

"I don't know who you are anymore. None of you. For the last several months, more I think, it's been a war between the six of you, and I've had enough. Don't push me, Nashville. If you do, I swear with all that is holy that there will be no saving you. I'm finished with you."

When she left, closing the door quietly behind her, Nash stood there for several long minutes, trying his best to get his temper under control. There was nothing he could do. So, wiping his hand over the top of his desk, he roared along with the sound of breaking glass, computer equipment, and whatever else was atop his desk.

His apartment wasn't any place he wanted to be, either. After tossing what was left of his briefcase and laptop in the back seat of his truck, gunning the motor, he left the parking garage and drove. Nash didn't care if he hit someone, got a ticket, or anything else happened on his way out of town, but lord help the person or persons that decided that they wanted to speak to him.

At noon, he pulled off the highway to get himself

something to eat. He wouldn't have bothered, but his head was slightly off, and his cat felt like he was chewing at his insides. Pulling into the first place, he saw that there weren't that many cars in the lot. He got out and went inside. As soon as he was told to seat himself, Nash knew that he should have left and used one of the million-and-one drive-thru places rather than having a face to face with anyone right now.

When he was handed a menu, Nash didn't bother looking at the person but stretched his neck, popping it several times before glancing at the water-stained menu and handing it back to the person.

"Don't speak to me. Ever. Just bring me two number ones and a pitcher of water with a glass of ice. No talking. No questions." He looked at his options. "Scrambled eggs, bacon and sausage, and hash browns."

The menu was snatched from his hand, and a few seconds later, a set of silverware wrapped in a paper napkin was slammed on the table in front of him. The glass of ice was next. Several of the slippery chunks went slithering across the table when two large pitchers of water joined the glass. He might have found it funny, but he got what he wanted and didn't care how the person's feelings were crushed.

Not bothering to look around, he sat at his booth and contemplated his mother's threat. There was no doubt that she would do as she said. When their father had slapped her around one night, they found his body cut to ribbons in the field next to the baseball field where he and his brothers had played ball. There was no doubt that he had suffered and badly. His father had been a bastard all their lives. But that night, he'd not taken his temper out on them but their mother.

The food arrived just as he was thinking that the waitress had decided to cut her losses and leave him to starve. He could only stare at the amount of food that was on both platters. There were several more, too, little bowls of fried apples and grits, as well as what smelled to him like apple butter. When he looked up to see if the waitress was going to give him anything else, she was already gone. While Nash was enjoying the first good homecooked meal he'd had in a decade, another pitcher was set in front of him, as well as two more glasses of ice. All delivered without word one spoken from her.

He was just finishing up his last biscuit. They seemed to endlessly appear on his table, and the check mysteriously appeared. Nash picked it up and looked at the total. There wasn't any kind of bastard fee, something that he'd had tacked onto his bill lately. No nasty remarks about taking his business elsewhere from now on. Just the cost of two of the platters, tax, and nothing else. Picking it up, he made his way to the cash register.

Full, he did seem to be in a much better mood, but nothing that wouldn't flare up again if provoked. And by provoking him, it would only take one misplaced word, and he'd be set off again. As soon as he reached for his wallet out of his back pocket, he knew he was going to be fucked. And with the way his temper was now at full force again, so would the person who was going to give him grief about him having to go to his truck to get his wallet. The woman who waited on him only took the bill from him and glared.

"I left my wallet in the truck." Before he could tell her that he'd go out and get it, she reached into the sunshine yellow apron she had on, pulled out twenty-five bucks, and rang him out. When she walked away, his rage made him nearly blind. "I have the fucking money. I said I left my wallet in the truck, not that I didn't have…where the fuck are you going? Come back here."

"Mister." He turned to look at the person behind him. "I don't think you should be talking to her like that. Sunny is a good girl, and she doesn't need you to be—"

"She paid my fucking bill." The elderly man backed away from him. "I didn't tell her that I didn't have the money. She had no right to pay it off when I was going out to get it."

"I heard you talking to her when you came into the restaurant. You just be glad that she didn't dump that water over your noggin. Get on out of here." He looked around the restaurant and could see that the odds were still in his favor because of him being a jaguar. There would be a lot of human deaths if he didn't leave right now. Even as he backed to the door, his temper getting hotter and hotter, he didn't say another word. Damn it, he was going to pay his bill.

Leaving the lot, he had to pull over again about a mile down the road. Nash couldn't see his head was so hot. Getting out of the truck, he made his way to the tree line and shifted. Mother fuck, whatever got into his path right now was going to be in trouble if they didn't stay the hell away from him.

~*~

"Sunny? You out here?" Sunny didn't answer Doris but stayed behind the dumpster where she'd been for the last half hour. Her shift had ended twenty minutes before the man had shown up. Once he spoke to her when she handed him the menu, she knew that he would have eaten alive anyone else that was around him. So she stayed to keep the peace.

The doors to the dumpster opened, and she was glad to see that it was Wayne, the busboy. He would dump the trash and not say a word to anyone so that he'd not have to use up any of his time right now to smoke. Why people still did that, even with all the reports going around about how bad it was for you, was beyond her.

Keeping hidden, she looked at the pitiful amount of money she still had in her hands after paying the man's bill and cried again. Her power was going to be turned off again. There was no hope for it. Even with her keeping everything off and not even using enough to cook herself a hot meal, her bill kept going up and up. The fourteen dollars that she'd made today, plus the extra ten that she'd been counting on to get eggs and milk, was all gone. Sunny hadn't a clue what she was going to do now but gathered up her things and left the little closed-off area where the large dumpster was locked in.

Walking home wasn't all that much of a hardship for her. She'd been walking since she'd gotten the job, and now was no different. Tomorrow, it was supposed to rain, so she'd been watching sales on umbrellas now but at the moment, she couldn't have afforded a newspaper had they been only a nickel.

Cutting through the trees to cut about three miles off her way home, she didn't bother looking around at the trees and other undergrowth. Sunny had worn a path through the trees and knew this way better than she did her own mind. As she was coming up to what she considered the halfway point, she felt herself being hit from the side and go tumbling ass over end deeper into the trees knocking her head against something hard.

Opening her eyes, she nearly screamed, finding a large black spotted cat standing over her. She knew that it wasn't a house cat. There wasn't any way that this sucker was anything but a jaguar. A wild cat had found her. His saliva was dripping off his long fangs and onto her face when she tried to scramble away from him. His large paw digging into her shoulder had her crying out and stopping when she hit her head again.

Opening her eyes again, this time, it was darker than she thought it should have been in the woods. Sunny could feel the blood as it poured from the wound. Lifting her chin when he went from beast to man, she looked into the very pissed-off eyes of the man in the diner this afternoon.

"Mine," he said as he tugged at her clothing.

"What the fuck are you talking about?" Sunny tried her best to wiggle from beneath him until he pulled both her hands up and over her head and held them there. The man said she was his mate. She didn't want to acknowledge it, but she couldn't deny the attraction either. She was as naked as he was when he ran his hand down her body.

"You're not going to scream? Not going to beg me to stop?" Not opening her mouth, not giving him at all what he wanted, she lifted her chin and glared at him. "Cute. Very cute."

His mouth lowered to hers, and she knew that he was going to kiss her. There was no way she was going to make this easy for him, mate or not. Each time he tried to pull her forward, she turn her face away from him. He surprised her by laughing, but when his mouth finally covered hers, she wanted to hate it, but she was lost in that heady kiss. And God help her. She wanted more.

Without another word, he filled her with his cock. Screaming behind her closed mouth, she felt her mouth fill with blood when she bit through her lips to keep from letting it go. She'd never had sex before. The pain, she knew, was more than normal, her body aching as he began to move in and out of her, and the more he moved, the more she wanted.

As he took his time with her, slowly fucking her, she tried her best not to move. Not to do anything that would have him thinking she was enjoying herself, too. His mouth suckled at her breasts, her throat, and ears. Sunny wanted to beg him for more, but she'd not give him the satisfaction. Not a sound from her if she could help it.

But, like him, her body betrayed her. She came so hard when he lifted her ass up to meet his downward thrusts that she screamed silently again. His laughter, chuckling like he'd won the grand prize, had her turning her head away from him and going limp.

When he finished, roaring out when he came, she didn't move when he let go of her hands and rolled away. As soon as she was free of his weight, Sunny rolled away from him, snatching up her clothing and running as fast as she could away and to the path where she'd been going home.

It took her several minutes to realize that he wasn't chasing her. Going back, only close enough that she could see that he was sleeping or unconscious, Sunny got close enough to get the rest of her things. Her apron that had her nametag on it, as well as her shoes. Keeping an eye on the fucker, she dressed quickly and went back to the path. She was standing on the path again when she remembered something about shifters.

He'd bitten her. Not only that, but she was sure that he'd taken a bit of her blood, too, when he'd done it. Sunny knew that he could follow her with what he had of hers and stood on the path again, trying to figure out how to get away.

Going back the way of the restaurant. She was still sobbing when the trash truck pulled in. After it emptied the dumpster and put it back in the locked space, she waited until the man was back in his truck, and then she hopped into the back of the truck. It smelled bad, gross really, but she knew, or at least she thought she knew, that if she wasn't on the ground, there was no way that he could find her. Christ, oh mighty, she hoped that was at least true.

As she lay there in the leftover food and nasty shit that had gone out in the trash today, she wondered why she'd even bothered. He'd gotten what he wanted, hadn't he? I mean, she didn't think he'd gotten a good fuck, but he had at least gotten his jollies. As she watched the sky speed past her on the way to wherever she was headed, Sunny cried harder than she had in a very long time.

She must have fallen asleep crying, so when she woke up, it took her a bit to remember what had happened. All she had to do was move, trying to get out of the truck to remember how he'd hurt her. How his claws had scrapped over her skin. His teeth had made marks on her. The places at her wrists where he'd held her hands above her head were already turning a deep blue. She couldn't imagine what her face might have looked like.

Finding herself outside of her apartment complex, she stood there waiting to cross the street when she saw his big truck pull into the drive to the complex. Backing away, keeping her eye on him, Sunny moved between the two buildings behind her and waited. It didn't take her long to see him get out of his truck, his temper no better it seemed than it had been earlier, and make his way into the front of the place.

Sunny knew that there was a policy about giving out personal information about the staff that worked at Good Morning. However, she also knew that enough money would get a person whatever they wanted about anyone. It wouldn't have surprised her to know that even the president could be paid off if there was enough cash involved. When the man came out of the front of her building and made his way to his truck, Sunny didn't move from her hiding place. Why he'd pay anything to know anything about her was a mystery, but then she wasn't going to question a pissed-off shifter.

Knowing that she couldn't go home, not that there was all that much there anyway, she backed between the buildings until she knew she was out of sight from anyone looking from the street. Finding herself an open door, she got herself inside and stayed in the darkness until her eyes adjusted. There were several rooms around her in the abandoned building, most of the ceiling had been taken down, but there were enough of the stairs for her to go up them when she paused on the first step.

He could still find her. Again, not sure why he'd care, but he had come this far. Sunny pulled her shoes off, leaving her socks on, and took some of the bits of trash that was around her and wrapped it over her feet, tucking it into her socks. Careful that she used what she touched, she made her way up the stairs. She wished that she owned a book about the shit there was out there about shifters. And if there was, she was going to get her a copy if it was the last thing she ever did. When she got to the second level, then the third, careful of touching anything, she made her way to the middle of the building and leaned against the wall as she sat. Every part of her body hurt.

Crying herself to sleep again, Sunny didn't know what she was going to do now. She'd really done nothing wrong, she told herself. But the big man had a bone to pick with her, and he wasn't stopping anytime today. Tomorrow, she told herself. Tomorrow, he'd move on, and she'd be back to waiting tables and keeping her distance from everyone from now on.

Waking up sometime in the darkest part of the night, Sunny heard rustling. Knowing that it was rats, she had some of her own in her own building, and she didn't move. Not that she thought that she could have. Her body had decided that whatever had been done to it was enough to kill her, and she was just waiting to die.

"Where the fuck are you?" Flitching at the sound of his harsh voice seeming so close to her, she cried out, scaring the rats and whatever else was around her away. *"Tell me where you are so that I can come and get you. Stop being fucking childish, and let me come and get you. I know that you are hurt. I can fucking feel it."*

Nearly answering the man, knowing that he wasn't as close as he sounded, she kept her mouth closed. That was when she remembered her lips and how she'd bitten through them. The pain was too much, and she felt herself nearly sliding away into unconsciousness. It took everything that she had to hold on. Unable to move at all, her hands and legs raw with pain, she lay there as quietly as she could while he continued to scream at her to tell him where she was.

"So you think to make me suffer, do you? I have news for you, Sunshine Nettles: I suffer for no one. So we had a good fuck, and it turns out that you're my mate. So the fuck what? Do you think that I'm going to come to you on bended knee and beg you for mercy? Not fucking

likely. Tell me where you are. I'll give you some cash, get you healed up, and then you can be on your fucking merry way. I don't have time for this shit." Her mind stilled at the fact that he'd said she was his mate again. *"You fucking bitch, tell me where you're hiding. I've been all over this city, and you're hiding from me. This isn't going to get you any brownie points with me. Nor are you going to be able to blackmail me into setting you up in some kind of fancy home with money and a car, either. I don't want you in my fucking life."*

It occurred to her that he'd never once asked her how badly she was hurting. Nor did he ask her if she needed anything from him. No, it was all about what she thought that she was going to take from him. She knew just what kind of man he was and decided that if she lay here and died, she'd be better off than she was anywhere near that man.

Sunny knew that she was losing blood. How much wasn't anything that she could think of right now. As she lay there, slipping in and out of consciousness, she was careful each time she woke that she was alone.

By the time the sun was bleeding through the windowless front of the building, Sunny knew that on a very bad level, she wasn't going to make it if she stayed here much longer. It didn't make her get up, even if she thought that she could, but she did look at herself. It made her sick and physically throw up when she saw the state of her arms. There wasn't a place on them that wasn't blue or bleeding. It must have all happened when the cat attacked her. It looked as if three of her fingers were broken, bent out of shape. Even her legs were beyond anything she'd ever seen before. Touching her fingers to the wound at her neck, Sunny couldn't have held the scream back if she'd been paid a million dollars.

"Don't move." She opened her eyes but thought that there was something wrong with at least one of them. Focusing was impossible, and she was sure that the woman next to her was as beautiful as any queen she'd ever seen in a book. "What a lovely thing to say to me. Thank you. But you just lay still, and I'm working on getting you some help."

Making her mouth move, she begged the woman to kill her. Sunny wanted that more than she had her next meal. Closing her eyes when she was told to, Sunny felt someone touch her arm, and she cried out. Even though it pained her to speak, she had to make this person understand something.

"He's after me. Please, kill me. I don't want

him to find me so that he'll finish the job. Please, he'll make me suffer." The woman said she had her. "I didn't do a thing to him. I did want what he wanted, and that was all." She heard the sharp intake of breath and thought it was her. There wasn't any way that anyone would care.

"I care. You're going to be all right, my dear. I swear to you." Sunny felt herself sliding away again. This time, she didn't fight it. If this was death, then she was fine with that. At least she wouldn't hurt anymore.

Chapter 2

Archie didn't know what this was all about, but being called back into the offices today wasn't something that he'd been planning on. As soon as he was seated, second to last to arrive, making sure that he was as far from his brothers as he could be, he reached for the pitcher of water and poured himself a large glass of it. It wasn't until Nash came in, his face a bloodied mess, that he realized that this was more than just some temper flaring. This was bad.

He leaned over to ask Nash what had happened to him when he snarled at him. He'd like to think that this was something new for his little brother, but they'd all been snarling and tearing into each other for months now. Sitting up in his chair again, draining the glass of water, he stood up with the others when their mother entered the room.

"Sit your asses down." They did. Everyone had heard about the fight that Nash and his mother had had. Even her telling him that she'd tear his throat out. Archie knew that if she had indeed said it, and looking at his brother, he had a thought that they'd tangled already, she would follow through. All the years that their father had been knocking them around, never touching their mother or them letting her know that he'd been doing it, had cost their sire his life. Archie had no doubt that their mother would do anything she set her mind to, including making one of them pay. "Eight days ago, your brother met his mate."

He didn't know who that might have been until Nash stood up. He asked their mother where she was, but all she did was dig her nails, a very vibrant shade of red, a good inch into the oak table they were all sitting at. Staring at the two of them, wondering what the fuck was going on, it wasn't until Nash made his way to the door that he thought things were going to get worse than he could have imagined.

"You go out that door, and I will have you arrested. Not only will you spend the rest of your life in prison, Nashville, but you will never be able to speak to any one of us again. And that would include that young woman. Sit your ass down or open the door. You decide. But know that there are eight officers on the other side of that door just hoping that you're going to be stupid enough to try and get by them." Nash didn't move, nor did their mother. "Come back to the table and sit down."

"Where is she?" Archie watched the two of them snarling words back and forth like a violent game of tennis. "I demand to know what she's told you too."

"Told me? She's not been able to say a word since I found her. She's been in a coma. Oh, and if you're interested, she has fifty-six stitches in her mouth. Five broken ribs, a broken wrist. Her ankle was so badly turned that they had to do surgery on it so that she could walk on it again. *If* she wakes up. Then there is the — Tell me something, Nashville, did you know she was a virgin when you took her? Or were you too fucking pissed off because she was nice to you to care." Nash turned, and he stood up when his brother took the few steps to their mother. "He's not going to hurt me, Archie. I think right now he's done enough hurting to last several lifetimes."

"You're only willing to hear her side of the

story." Mother told Nash again that she'd not spoken to the girl. She was still in a coma. "Like I'm supposed to believe you. How did you find her anyway if she was in a coma? Did she call you? Tell you that I hurt her? She enjoyed it as much as I did, and if she ever tells you any different, then she's a liar, too."

The fist came out of nowhere and knocked his brother back several feet. It took his mind a few seconds to realize that it hadn't come from his mother as he had first thought, but her father. Grandda looked about as pissed off as he'd ever seen him. The usual very friendly and affable man was gone. And in his place was a man who looked ready to go toe to toe with anyone that bothered his daughter. And that would include his grandson.

"You come near your mother again with that look in your eyes, and she won't have to have you killed. I'll do it all on my own." Nash didn't move off the floor but lay there staring at them with hatred in his eyes. "You'll sit your ass right there where she told you, or so help me, Nash, there will not be a hole deep enough for you to hide in. That little girl you hurt has already died twice since I've seen her. You killed off your own mate. How do you feel about that? If not for your momma finding her when she did, there would have been no saving her at all for you."

"I didn't ask for her to come into my life." Grandda took a step toward Nash, but he pushed him out of the way to get to him first. Knowing that he had a bit more magic than his younger brother, being firstborn, he lifted him up over his head and tossed him across the room and into the fireplace that graced the other wall.

Breathing hard, he glared at Nash. Waiting and hoping that he'd come at him. When he stayed where he was, a crumbled mess on the floor, Archie went to him and pulled him up from the floor. Shoving him across the room, he put him in the chair he'd been in and stood behind him, holding him in place with his paws biting deeply into his flesh.

"I'm not going to ask you where she is because it's frankly none of his business. But is there anything we can do to keep her safe?" Grandda told him that it was up to the young woman right now if she lived or died. "I take it that she doesn't want to."

"She begged me to kill her when I found her so that Nashville couldn't find her and make her suffer more." Digging his claws deeper into his brother, he felt him wince at the pain. It mattered little to Archie if he suffered or not right now. His mate, whoever she was, wasn't going to be treated this way again. After Mom told them all the story about how he'd come to meet his mate and then finding out later what else he'd done to her, each of the others wanted to stand behind Nash, too. Archie didn't know why he cared but he thought that Nash might live longer if it was him there. The others were out for his blood, and he didn't think they'd stop at that.

"This isn't all on me. I told her that I left my wallet in the truck. If she'd not paid, then I wouldn't have gotten pissed off." Archie looked at Weston when he laughed. It was Nash that spoke to him. "What? You think I'm funny? I didn't do anything wrong. I told her that I'd pay."

"I don't doubt that you would have. What I think is funny is that you said you'd not have gotten pissed off at her. You've gotten us all pissed off and in the same mood as you are, and we're not mated to you. I cannot imagine what that little girl thought when you held her down with all your shifter strength and made her *pay* for being a nice person. How much was the bill, Nash? Millions of dollars? I'm betting that whatever it was, it was more than she could afford." Mom told them what had happened at her apartment. "So, she paid your bill instead of paying her heat bill, and you didn't think that a simple thank you would have been better? Christ, Nash, if she never has another thing to do with you, you'll be fucking lucky. Did it ever occur to you that, as your mate, you could have gotten her with child?"

"She'd better not fucking try and tell anyone that I impregnated her. I'll tear her throat out." Archie had enough. Giving his brother another squeeze to hurt him more, he let go and left the room. He wasn't going to be there when Nash figured out what he was doing.

Going home, he couldn't think beyond what his brother was doing. Archie let his cat take him as soon as he was in his yard. He'd not had a good run in longer than he could remember and thought that it might be some of the problems he was having. That and being around Nash. As soon as he made his way to his house, going inside naked, he didn't bother covering himself up when he realized that he had company. Grandda might fuss at him, but he'd not make a big deal out of him being naked in his own home.

After telling the old man he'd be back that he was going to take a shower. After trying his best to wash his anger off himself, Archie dressed in some jeans and a tee and didn't bother with socks and shoes. Again, it was his house and his rules. Grandda was on the phone when he entered the kitchen where he was.

"All right then. Yes." Grandda looked at him as he held the cell to his ear. "Has she asked for anything? Anything at all?" After another pause and his grandda looking about as crestfallen as he'd seen anyone, he told the person on the other end to call him if there were any changes.

"She's awake, I take it." Grandda just nodded. Archie could almost feel his hurt. "What's going to happen to her now? I'm assuming that she won't be welcomed to the family anytime soon."

"I welcomed her. Even though I was not able to talk to her, I welcomed her to the family. Nothing that was done to her was a bit her fault. He killed her off as surely as if he'd put a bullet in her head. Now she's laying there in that big hospital bed with nary a person around her because she has been hurt by one of mine." Archie hurt for her, too. Even not thinking about the fact that his brother had done this to her, she was still a person. "I'm headed over there in a bit. Your momma, she doesn't want any of us being there too many times. She's afraid that — I can't believe that I'm going to say this, but she's afraid that Nash will find her. What is wrong with him?"

"I don't know, Grandda. I just don't know." The two of them picked around at some of the lunch he'd made the two of them. After shoving it away, he asked him how Mom had been able to find the girl. He realized then that he didn't know her name, not a thing about her.

"There isn't a person in this state that doesn't know who the six of you are. And who your mom is. When there was trouble that morning at this little diner about an hour from here, someone called her and told her that Nash had been in and hadn't paid his bill. It'd been taken care of, of course, but the owner of the place wanted LouCinda to know that it had cost the girl all her money for the day. She headed over there right away to make things right." Archie asked if she really had just paid the bill. "Never said a word either. Of course, when Nash sat down, he told her to shut up and to bring him his food. That's what she did, too. Never giving him bad service either, but making sure that he had biscuits when he was done with them and full pitchers of water, too. By the time LouCinda got there, they'd heard all about him looking for Sunny, that's her name, Sunshine Nettles, and that someone had seen her jumping in the trash truck when it came by. It didn't take your mom long to figure out where the next stop was and that Sunny had gotten out there. By then, she'd been hurt. It wasn't until she found her that she realized that Nash had taken her, too. She was in poor shape, your mom told me. Just in terrible shape. Lost a lot of blood. When she begged your mom to kill her, it broke something in your momma that I don't know that she'll ever recover from."

Deciding to go with his grandda to see the girl, Archie wasn't the least bit surprised to find that the young woman was staying in a homeless shelter. One of the rooms there had been converted into a state-of-the-art medical unit and had round-the-clock doctors and nurses. She was getting the best of care, for which he was happy to know, and when he sat down next to the bed, he could smell that she'd recently been drugged, too.

Picking up one of her hands, he couldn't believe how badly she was bruised even after all this time. Up and down her entire arm, there were bite marks as well as finger imprints too. His anger at his brother doubled when she opened her eyes and looked at him with fear.

"I'm not him." She still tried to get away from his holding her. Archie stood up and backed as far away from the bed as he could. "I'm going to let you go, Sunny. But please don't hurt yourself. I'm not Nash, but his brother, Archibald. Everyone just calls me Archie. I won't hurt you. I swear to you on my life that I won't hurt you."

"They told me that I was safe here." Her voice, raw and full of fear, was low. He could hear her, but it still hurt how much pain she was in. Again, assuring her that she was safe there, he asked her if she needed anyone called. "I don't have anyone around me anymore. There is no one for me to call and take care of me."

Archie wanted to tell her that she had five brothers. A mother and a grandda too. Even though his brother had done this to her, she still was their sister. As her eyes drifted closed, her body sliding under again, Archie sat there and let the tears fall down his face. Christ, this was not the way it was supposed to be when one of their kind found their other half.

When grandda joined him, he couldn't speak around the large lump that had formed in his throat.

Archie knew that he'd not had a thing to do with her being in the shape that she was in, but he felt guilty for her pain and suffering. Each time she moved and cried out, he ached even more for her. Wanting to find his little brother and make him hurt as much as he'd done to his mate, had him sitting with her until the sun came up the next morning. Terrified to leave and run into his brother, Archie stayed right where he was.

~*~

Nash hadn't left his apartment since he'd been called into a meeting with his mother two weeks ago. The walls of the place had suffered badly from his self-imposed confinement. He'd allowed his cat to have at it when he realized that he wasn't getting anyone to come to him. No delivery service would come to bring him shit once they heard his name and address. Since he owned the entire building, even using a different address got him nothing.

His brothers had washed their hands of him, too. Stretching his neck, he blamed that on his mother. She'd done this to him by butting her nose in where it wasn't any of her concern. Looking around, just on the off chance that she had heard his thoughts, he moved the broken couch to the dumpster that he'd brought his busted table and chairs to yesterday.

As it was now, he didn't have any furniture to speak of but a mattress. And it was in terrible shape, too. A single plate, though, he had nothing to put on it and some books that he'd not torn to shreds when he'd woken from a rage two days ago. Since then, he'd not had any more outbursts, but that didn't feed him or entertain him. He'd never owned a television, so that wasn't a hardship for him. Though he thought he might enjoy one with nothing else to occupy his mind.

"Having fun?" Nash ignored his brother Wrangler when he spoke to him from just outside the dumpster area. He hadn't noticed him when he'd gone out of his place, so he figured that he'd just shown up to torment him. Although, for the last twenty-four hours or so, he didn't think anyone could torment him as much as his own thoughts had been. He asked him what he wanted. "Mom thought you'd be hungry about now. I'm to tell you that she had nothing to do with no one wanting to bring you shit. She said that the entire town has you on their shit list because of your treatment of them when you call in."

He'd heard that, too. Not that he wasn't still

putting the blame on his mom, but he asked Wrangler what he'd brought him. He told him that he was going to take him out to dinner if he could behave himself.

"Why would you want to be seen with me? I don't know if you remember or not, but I'm a mate abuser and a bastard." Wrangler told him that he did remember that but didn't want him to suffer without food. There were other things that he thought he could suffer with more. "Gee, thanks."

Nash had showered just before taking the couch out. He knew that before that, it had been a few days since he'd even brushed his teeth. It had been in his head to make others suffer for their treatment of him, but not brushing his teeth or showering hadn't bothered anyone but himself. So, taking a shower, washing his hair four times, he'd brushed his teeth that many times, too. He'd had a funk about him that even he couldn't stand.

He didn't want a big meal. He would have eaten it had they gone to a nice restaurant, but when his brother suggested burgers, his mouth watered for them. Nash was happy when they went through a drive-thru. He was not sure that he'd be fit to be next to people anymore. They sat in the parking lot and ate them without saying a word. They were on their way back to his place when he turned Wrangler.

"I don't have anywhere for you to sit down." He told him that he was only feeding him; he didn't want to be around him. For the first time in longer than he could remember, Nash felt a pain in his chest like his heart was breaking. When they pulled into his parking lot, as soon as he got out of Wrangler's truck, his brother sped away like the hell hounds were after him. Alone again, Nash made his way to his place again.

Dragging his mattress to the living room, he pulled out his laptop and began looking over some of the houses that he owned. If he was honest with himself, he was sick of his own company, and if he didn't get out of his place soon, he was going to leap over the edge of his patio as his cat and make sure that he was seen by every cop in the land so he could be arrested. At least in jail, he figured that someone would have to speak to him. If only to ask him what the hell he'd been thinking. He needed a house.

While he figured that having a house was just making him have more than the walls that he had now, Nash did think about Sunshine, too. He was going to have to get her something to live in. Trying his best not to think about living in the house with her, he was going to find her a home fit for royalty so that he could do one thing right for the young woman.

Nash had had a long time to think about his actions. Not just what he'd done to Sunshine but the weeks and months leading up to the day he'd found her. There was no doubt in his mind that he'd been a bastard to everyone. If his cell phone never ringing was any indication by not ringing with people asking about him, he didn't know what else to compare it to. No one, not his family, colleagues, nor even his own attorney, had once tried to contact him in any way.

After the third time of his brothers showing up to take him to dinner, he stopped going with them. Then, after a few days of telling them that he didn't want to go, he stopped opening the door to them, too. Now, if he was lucky, he got to go to the mailbox out of his apartment and saw someone. Not that he was feeling sorry for himself. No, it was just the opposite.

He didn't have anyone at all to blame for what he was dealing with now but himself. At what point, he couldn't have pinpointed it that he'd turned into the man that everyone hated. But the last month, he'd realized that he was totally to blame for everything.

Picking up his cell, after putting it off for a week, he called his personal attorney.

"Mr. Sheppard." The coldness of Rick's voice, like that of other people that he spoke to, hurt him. Rick and he had gone to grade school together. Had been good friends. Never once had he called him Mr. anything. Now, he was going to be reduced to beg the man for his forgiveness. It was no less than he deserved. "What is it I can do for you? I've got a very busy schedule of meetings today."

"I understand. I was wondering if you could come to my apartment this evening so that I can go over a few things." Rick told him that he set aside his time in the evening for his family. "Good. You should do that. Then can you clear a morning for me? The sooner, the better, but I don't want you to make any sacrifices to your schedule for me."

There was silence at the other end, and Nash was sure that he'd hung up on him. Again, it was no less than he deserved, and Nash knew that he'd have to find himself another attorney if his friend decided to wash his hands of him, too.

"Who is this?" Nash told him again who he was. "Yeah, well, I'd like to believe that. I would, but I also know that Nash Sheppard doesn't bend himself around anyone's schedule. I don't know what you're playing at, sir, but—"

"I know that I've said some things to you that were hurtful. I also know that I hurt you when I said something about your family, telling you that you needed to ditch them in favor of working for me. When I think of a lot of things that I've said to people over the last…I don't know how long I want to bury my head in a hole and never come out. You have no idea how sorry I am…well, for everything. This is me, Rick. I swear to you that I'm trying my best to make amends to a lot of people, but I need you to help me. I…I was going to tell you what happened, but I'm sure you've heard."

"You hurt your mate." He said that he did, reaching for his tissues when he thought of Sunshine and wiped at his tears. "It's also said that your family won't have anything to do with you."

"They won't. Not that I blame them for that, either. But I do have a mate and even if she never wants to see me, I'd like to make her life a good deal better than I have so far. I need someone to help me. A friend to help me, and the first person that I thought of was you." He blew his nose, not even embarrassed that he was sobbing again. "The things that I did to her, Rick, I just don't know who that person was. My mom threatened to kill me. She would have, too, I have no doubt. And there have been times when I think of myself that I wish she had. I've spent the last month getting to know the bastard that I was and working hard at trying to be the man that Sunshine could be happy about. I'm not saying I want to do this to *make* her want to be around me. She deserved more than me. Hell, everyone in the world deserves more than me. Can you help me? Please? I need to set her life up, one without me, so that she can go on living."

"What do you mean, go on living? Are you planning something stupid?" He told his former friend that he'd been stupid for a very long time. "Yes, I can tell you that I agree with that, but what do you plan on doing once I have this young woman set up?"

"I don't know." That was the honest truth, too. He didn't know what he was going to do once Sunshine was taken care of. "I just know that she needs something that I can provide for her, and there is no reason for her to do without simply because I'm her mate."

"I don't know if I can make this work with

you, but I'll try. If I can't work with you, I'll let you know right away so that you can find someone else. And I will agree with you, too, on that she could do a lot better than having you as her mate." Nodding, knowing that Rick couldn't see him, had him reaching for more tissues. "I'll have to call you back in an hour. It'll take some work to get your files out of storage and clear my day for tomorrow. However, one nasty word from you and you'll be out on your ass so fast that what your family is doing to you will look like a day in the park. Do I make myself clear?"

"Yes. Very much so. Thank you. So much." He cleared his throat, thinking of the list of things that he'd been working on the last few weeks. "I'll wait for your call. Thank you, Rick. Very much again."

Putting his cell down, he curled into the pillow that he'd gotten yesterday and laid down. He'd been a fool. He still might be, but he was going to make things right if it killed him. And someone might be out there right now plotting his demise, and Nash thought that he'd welcome it with open eyes.

At just after ten, he got up and got himself cleaned up. He'd heard twice from Rick. Once, to tell him that he would see him tomorrow and then again to set things up for him with the bank. That had been the most difficult thing for him to get finished. The banker hadn't wanted him anywhere near the bank for any reason.

For the past week, he'd been going to sit in the room with Sunshine just to watch her sleep. Finding out where she'd been staying had been quite a bit of work, but now that he found her, he wanted to make sure that she was safe, especially from men like him.

Sitting in the chair in her room, he thought about what the nurse had told him about her being released tomorrow. While he had an idea where she might be headed, he was still afraid that he'd not be able to see her again. These last nights with her, just being close to her, he knew that it was more than he could have hoped for. When she suddenly sat up in her bed and looked right at him, Nash knew that he was going to end up in prison before the night was over. He was just glad that he'd been able to write out what he had wanted done for her so that she'd be taken care of.

"I don't want you here." He nodded and stood up. "Why are you here anyway? If you come at me again, one of your brothers, who I like, by the way, gave me a gun to use on you. I might not be able to kill you, but I will make you suffer."

"It's no less than I deserve." She didn't move, and he didn't either. "I'm sorry. It seems to be so inadequate, but I am. Also, if you would contact someone for me after I leave, I'd appreciate it."

He left her there. Nearly to the elevators, he didn't turn when he felt the bite of the gun to his back. He knew it was Sunshine. He could smell her. Nash put up his hands and told her not to go to prison for him. He would leave her alone.

When the elevator opened, he stepped inside. Not turning, not wanting to have his last image of her with a gun pointed at him, he stayed where he was and heard the doors close behind him.

Chapter 3

Sunny knew she was making a mistake when she stepped into the elevator with Mr. Sheppard. When he turned and looked at her, she backed into the furthest corner away from him and was surprised when he did the same.

"What's the matter with you?" He asked her what she meant. "I don't fucking know. When I met you the first time, you were a rude bastard who didn't want anyone to speak to you. 'Just bring the food and shut up,' man. Now you look like…who knocked you around anyway? If you tell me that I did that, I'm going to shoot you."

"Some of my family did it." When he didn't say anything else, she grabbed him by the ear and dragged him down to the room she'd been in. Never once did he fight with her or demand that she let him go, which sort of worried her. When she did let him go and slammed the door behind them, he stared at her before speaking. "I'm trying my best here to figure out what it is you want me to do. First, you pull a gun on me, then you drag me down the hall to your room."

"I don't know what I want either." She told him to sit down, and he did. That pissed her off as well. "You're all…you're like a domesticated cat that has had all its meanness pulled out of it, and now he doesn't know what to do with himself. Or is it… you're here because of something your family said. Like that you were to come here and be nice to me. Something along the lines of if you didn't, you'd not be welcome to them to allowing you to be around anymore."

"No." He stretched his neck and then apologized. "Yes, they're mad at me. All of them. My mom especially, and more than my next breath, I want to make it up to her. However, this has very little…no, it has all to do with you, and I'm trying to fix it all the way around. I've been—"

"Are you saying that this is all my fault? I'll have you know that I did just what you told me to do and didn't have an issue with it. Well, I did, but

I didn't get pissy with you about it. Then when you didn't have the money for your bill—to be honest, I was feeling guilty and remorseful about how I had treated you. However, since you'd already been so nice and friendly about me not speaking to you—that's sarcasm if you don't get it, I couldn't explain to you why I was doing it. Then you hit me." He asked her when he'd hit her. "When you came out of the woods. You ran me down while I was on my way home."

"I didn't run you down." She said that he had. Sunny explained to him that she'd been on the path and that she'd been bowled over by him. Then he stood over her as his great cat like he was going to eat her alive. "You were already…when I found you in the forest, you were alone and partly naked and unconscious. Yes, there were scratches on your skin. A wound…I didn't look at it, but I could smell that cat from the diner on you, so I assumed that…What did my cat look like? I mean, you saw the cat that ran you down, I'm assuming? Was he dark or a light-colored fur?"

Suddenly, her knees gave out on her, and if not for Mr. Sheppard leaping forward and catching her, she might well have fallen to the floor. He picked her up, carrying her to the bed when all she could think about was that the cat that had stood over her had been dark, his eyes a shade of brown that looked black. Sunny looked at the man who might well have recused her twice since she'd met him.

"What color are you?" He told her that he was a tawny color, all his family were. "And your eyes, they're not brown but a very dark blue. Your eyes are blue, not brown."

Someone was holding her down with her head between her knees on the bed. Sunny was sure that at some point she'd fainted, realization coming at her hard, but all she could think of was the color of the eyes of the other cat that had knocked her to the ground.

Sunny looked at the window that she knew wasn't there before. Sitting up on the bed, she also realized that she was no longer in the hospital but a home. With beautiful colored curtains that matched the spread she was lying on perfectly. The yellow in the room, along with the other warm colors, made the room a perfect place to take a nice nap and —

Getting out of the bed before she started acting like an idiot and taking a long nap, she realized that she wasn't the only person in the room, but Mr.

Sheppard was there with her. Poking him in the shoulder had him coming awake quickly and pulling her body flush to his. Neither of them moved, Sunny waiting for whatever dream she'd woke the man from was fogging up his head.

"Did I hurt you?" She said that he'd not, but he still held her. "I was having a terrible dream, and when I jumped up, I have a cramp in my back. I must have slept in the chair oddly, and now I can't move. Just...will you please not scream or anything and give me a minute to let it stretch out?"

"Of course." She would never admit this to anyone, but it was nice having someone holding her like this. Not allowing herself to think about him having a bad dream that had brought him to holding her. When the muscles in his arm, the one that was holding her under her breasts, started to relax, Sunny stayed right where she was until he was ready. "I don't know where I am. It's lovely, but I haven't any idea how I got here or where...I'm babbling. I'm sorry."

"It's all right. You're at my mother's home. Once I figured out what had happened in the woods behind the diner, I realized how unsafe it was for you to be at the homeless center. The man that hurt you knew where you were before I did. Did he visit you?" She asked him who that might be. "I'm sorry. The dishwasher, Peter Burk. It didn't occur to me that he was the one until you mentioned that I hurt you in the forest. I did...I did take you. But I didn't hurt you the first time. When I came upon you, like I said, you were already bleeding and half naked. I think his intentions were to rape and then kill you."

"Peter is an old man." He removed his arms from her, but she could tell, almost feel he was still in pain. "I didn't even know he was a cat until...what is it you're saying to me? That Peter was going to rape me? That can't be right."

The door to the bedroom opened, and she felt Nash's sadness. There was anger there as well, but not like his sadness. When his mother stepped into the room, Nash walked to the furthest wall and leaned against it. For some reason, Sunny's heart broke for the man.

"My son is right, I'm afraid. Peter was arrested this morning, just after my son brought you here so you'd be safe. He was arrested for murder, rape, and a long list of other things. Some are only just coming to light, I'm afraid." Mrs. Sheppard, whom she had met the day she'd been found, sat down in the large wingback chair and asked her to do the same. She noticed that Nash stayed where he'd moved to and didn't acknowledge him at all. Sunny noticed, too, that she was referring to him only as her *son* and not by his name. "I have some information for you, Sunny. However, until the trial, you can't tell anyone what it is you already know about the other man. If not for you speaking to him about his cat, Sunshine, there is no telling how much longer this man would have gone on his spree of raping and killing young women such as yourself. He's been working at the diner for two decades. And in that time, eleven waitresses have come up missing as well as eight more have been linked to the same man. The police had no idea that the man they were looking for was right under their noses."

"He's a cat too then." Even though she'd been looking at Nash for answers, it was his mother that answered her. "What's going on here?"

"I told you, I had some information for you. I do have more if you would allow me to speak. It's only through you that this is all coming to light, and the police wish to speak to you about it." She asked about Nash. "What about him?"

"Why are you not speaking to him too?" She

looked at Nash, who still hadn't said a word, even to his mother, in the way of greeting. The sadness was still there, but she could also feel a twinge of anger. "Without his help, I would have gone on thinking that he's the one who tried to kill me out there by knocking me around. It wasn't him. Not all of it, anyway. Yet you're acting as if he's not standing right there."

"I'm mad at him." She asked her what she had to be mad at him about. "Well, he had his way with you, or did you forget about that. Then there was the way that he treated you afterwards too. He's not been to see you once."

"Yes, he has. Several times." She didn't know how many other than the night before he'd shown up. The nurse had hinted that someone special was coming to see her, but she didn't give her his name. "Also, he brought me here to keep me safe. I don't know how you think that would have worked out if he'd not been there talking to me. Then there is the fact that, as I said, he's standing right there."

"That is none of your concern." Sunny glared at the woman, and when she stood up, so did Sunny. "Look here, young lady. I'm trying to save you from yourself. He abused you and hurt you badly."

"But that's not true either, is it? He didn't hurt me at all. Other than...he didn't rape me. I enjoyed it as much as he did." The slap to her face startled her. When the woman looked as if she was going to hit her again, Sunny found herself behind Nash and him standing toe to toe with his mother. "As you can see, Mrs. Sheppard, he has better manners than you do right now. Why the hell did you hit me?"

"You'll learn your place, Sunshine." She said that her name was Sunny. "It's not, really. Is it? I despise shortened versions of names. The only reason that I have allowed Archie to get by with his is because his father had the same name as Archibald, and it was too much confusion. Nashville, go back over there and let Sunshine and I work this out."

"No." She had a feeling that Nash had never stood up to his mom before. And if he had, he'd paid for it dearly. "I'm going to take my mate, Sunny, home with me. It was a mistake to bring her here."

She didn't fight with him when he asked her if she could please get her shoes. Nor did she say a word when he took her hand into his much larger one to guide her out of the room. As soon as they were in the hall, several men stood at the bottom of the flight of stairs, all of them with their hands on their guns that were strapped to their sides.

Something was off here. While she could see some of the anger that was coming from Mrs. Sheppard, she couldn't understand her demanding things of her son. Her either, for that matter.

"My son is taking this woman against her will, and I want you to stop them." Sunny moved so that she was going down the stairs first, in front of Nash. "Make sure that you don't hurt her, please. She's my daughter-in-law."

"I'm not being taken anywhere I don't want to go." Mrs. Sheppard told the men that Nash had talked her into saying that. "All right then, we'll have to settle this the old-fashioned way. I'm going to call the police if you detain me for any reason as I move out of this house. Mrs. Sheppard is the one who is holding me against my will, and if you assist her, I will press charges against the lot of you and own everything you have by the end of the day. I might only be a waitress, but I'm a smart one who is working her way through college to become the best attorney in the land. Either part ways so that we can leave or face the consequences of the police."

The one that seemed to be in charge laughed. She might well have, too, facing a man and a woman with a very wealthy woman behind them spewing lies. Looking at Nash when he said her name, she took the cell phone from him. Her first priority was to get them out of the house. Then she'd be calling the police if that didn't work. Dialing the only number that she'd ever used, Sunny called her father's mom.

"Hello, Jackson. It's Sunshine Nettles. I was wondering if I could speak to the lady of the house, please? I know it's been a while, but—" Jackson told her that her grandmother was in the garden and he'd tell her that she had a call. "Don't bother her if she has company. I can call her later."

"Nonsense. I have her right here." Closing her eyes, Sunny tried to think when it was the last time that she'd actually spoken to Antebellum Nettles and realized that it had been since her parents had died. Eight years ago. After a short exchange of Jackson telling Belle that she had a call, she heard her laughing before she said her greetings.

"It's Sunny, Belle. I'm sorry to bother you, but I have a slight problem here, and I need someone to come and get myself and my mate." The scream was loud and piercing. Even Nash backed away from the phone when she did that. "You don't have to come yourself, but if you could send Jackson to—"

"And allow him to have all the fun. I think not. Tell me where you are." She handed the phone to Nash so that he could tell her. While she couldn't hear what Belle was saying, she knew that someone would come there soon. Handing her back the phone, Nash was smiling for the first time since she'd met him. "The Sheppard's, huh? Well, that's not what I expected to find out today. Jackson is getting the car revved up, and we'll be there soon. It's been a while, Sunny. I hate that you've decided to call me because you're in trouble. We'll have to remedy that soon, don't you think?"

"I'll do whatever you wish if you get me out of this house all in one piece." Laughter again, and then the line went dead. Handing the phone back to Nash, she told him that they were to wait for her to arrive.

It occurred to her then that she'd not told her grandmother why she needed out of the house. Nor did she ask. While she didn't know her grandmother all that well, very little, as a matter of fact, she was grateful for her help in this. There was more going on here than just a simple family being mad at another family member.

~*~

Nash only spoke when someone asked him a question. He was focusing all his energy on keeping an eye on Sunny. While they'd not moved off the stairs, still between the standoff, he had to admit that she was much more beautiful than he had remembered. When he'd met her, hurt her, she'd already been bruised up and bleeding. Someone was going to pay for that, too, he told himself.

The front doorbell rang, and his mom told Billings, her butler, not to answer it. Nash hadn't thought of his mother not allowing Sunny's grandmother to come into the house. But when it exploded back, breaking not just the door itself and the hand-made glass mosaics down both sides of it and the table that had stood in the middle of the room for as long as he could remember. Even the flowers that were replaced daily went scattering when the police, about a dozen of them, came into the room with flack jackets and headgear on, but their weapons were drawn as well. They were all pointed at the men who were detaining them at the bottom of the stairs, as well as his mother.

"Hello, darling." Sunny told the very beautiful woman standing just inside the broken door mess she was glad to see her. "I would imagine that you are. You must be Nash, young man. Come here, the two of you. These men are going to be arrested. You are pressing charges, aren't you, Sunny?"

"Yes. I am. On his mother, too." Sunny looked at him, and he could see her concern. "If that's all right with you, Nash?"

"You go on and do what you need to do." Sunny stared at him for several seconds, and he nodded at her. "Press charges, Sunny. Please. It's no less than she deserves."

Nash watched his mother being taken out in cuffs. It was a thrilling sight to him but one he knew that he was going to pay for. His mother would not take kindly for having to be arrested in the first place, but to be dragged out of her own home in cuffs where the neighbors could see would put her over the edge. Mrs. Nettles, she'd asked him to call her Belle, asked the staff to bring them some light snacks as well as drinks to the dining room.

"And by drinks, I mean something that will burn our throats as it goes down. Understand?" They all looked at him as if he might be the one in charge now that their mistress had been taken away. Telling them it was fine got them moving, but he would have to get in touch with his brothers. He wondered if they'd want him arrested, too, for being such a prick to their mother. "You're afraid of her, aren't you, young man? Your mother, I mean. You're afraid of her."

"I wasn't until recently." He could have told her a lot of things, but she seemed all right with that answer. "I have to contact my brothers, too. I don't know how they'll take having Mother arrested, much less by me. I've not been on the good list here for a while now."

"It'll be fine, Nash. If they give you any more shit, I'll adopt you, and you won't have to deal with them anymore." Belle looked around the room they were in. "If this isn't a smash it in your face, I have money house, I don't know what else it could be called. Nash looked around then, too.

When he left Belle and Sunny to reach out to his brothers, he decided to do it privately and all of them at the same time. He hadn't any idea where his grandda was, but he was sure as soon as he found out, he'd be bailing his daughter out of jail. Which meant that he didn't have much time to get out of town. As surely as he was standing on the back deck of his mother's home, he knew that the old man would waste no time in coming after him.

After explaining to them all that had happened with Sunny when he'd been with her last night, he went on to tell them about how they'd ended up here instead of in his own home. Nash didn't explain how he didn't have anything to keep Sunny safe, but they all seemed to understand that he thought she'd be safer where they were. Then he told them how their mother had pulled in guards to keep them from leaving the house, as well as how there were guns pointed at them. The silence at the other end of the call made him nervous. It was Archie who spoke first.

"Did she hurt either of you?" It wasn't a question that he had anticipated, but he did tell his brother that she'd not, not physically, anyway. *"I'm in my truck now. I don't know where the rest of you are, but I'd like it if you were to meet us at the house. There are some things that I've been able to uncover, and I need…please? Will you all meet me at the family home?"*

They all agreed, and he reached out to Archie alone. When he told him that he'd explain when he arrived, he also said something else that startled Nash. He told him that he was profoundly sorry for the way that he'd been treated over the last few years. Going back into the dining room with Sunny and Belle, Nash missed what was being said to him. His mind was so messed up.

"Are you all right?" He turned and looked at Sunny and realized that it was just the two of them in the room. "You looked freaked out or something."

"I think that I am." He turned in the chair and looked at her, telling her everything that had been said when he had spoken to his brothers. "I have to tell you, Nash, I think your mom is a manipulative bitch that is used to getting her own way about shit and doesn't mind throwing her weight around to make sure that things go the way that she wants."

"It's funny you should say that. I have been sitting here thinking the same thing. Even though I messed up with taking you that day, I hadn't hurt you like she put out there that I had. If I were a father to someone who had supposedly done something like she said I'd done, I would have investigated a bit more before doing what—she turned my family against me and made sure that I didn't have contact with any of them. And this is something that really bothers me: she was going to kill me. I had to ask around, but she shouldn't be able to do that. Threaten? Yes. But she can't just kill me like she did our father." Sunny asked him why he thought she was doing that.

"Control? I don't know. But it has to be something. I don't understand why she is controlling us the way that she has been. And I think it's been our entire lives."

"I don't know her that well, but I'd say that she's used to getting things done the way that she wants them, and if you fuck up, then...she would have known that I was a waitress. Do you suppose she did this to keep us apart? I'm not saying that I want to hang out with you all that much, but why would she care if, as mates, the two of us got together? She hid us away from each other. Why? You could have healed me, right? But I was stuck in that—I did get good care, don't get me wrong there. But your brothers came to see me at night the way that you did." He nodded at her question, but the more he thought about it, the more questions that he had.

The doorbell rang, and he realized right then that it wasn't an appropriate ring for a house. It was a theme song from a movie about a child that had been possessed by the devil. Right off the top of his head, he couldn't remember the name of it, but he was sure that was what it was. When his brothers came into the dining room, Belle joined them, too. Behind her, the staff was bringing in drinks and platters of food for them to munch on. Their dinner, they were told was being catered in soon.

"All right, Sunny and gentlemen, I have a bit of news for you all. I don't know you at all, so when you have a question, I'd like for you to please tell me your name." Belle looked at him. "Nash, your mother is a fucking cunt, and the sooner that you and the others realize that, you might be better men than you are now."

Archie laughed. He was sure that he was laughing a bit too hard at hearing someone call his own mother a cunt, but when he stood up and hugged Belle, Nash wasn't sure what to do. This was the freakiest thing he'd ever witnessed in all his life.

"Ms. Nettles, you couldn't have said it any better." Archie looked around the table and then back at him. "Nash, I said this to you earlier, and I want to say it again in front of everyone. I am more sorry than I could ever be for treating you the way that I did. You messed up, hell, which one of us hasn't? But instead of pulling together like a family and trying to resolve anything to get the two of you on better starting ground, we treated the two of you like you had murdered our entire family and were ready and willing to walk away without finding out the truth.

I beg you for your forgiveness." He then turned to Sunny. "You, too, were a victim in all this. My brother did hurt you and treated you like shit, but there was no reason at all for us to have treated you like we did. Sneaking in to see you at night. Making sure that you had whatever you needed when we visited you. That is no way to treat someone. Especially not our newest family member."

Sunny got up and hugged each of his brothers. When she sat down next to him again, he braced himself for whatever she was about to say. He was sure that she was going to tell him to fuck off and to leave her alone. Instead, she took his hand into hers.

"I hate that I went along with everything like you were this terrible person. You did hurt me, but not physically. My heart was broken too if I'm honest, but it wasn't because of you, not all of it. If not for the staff where I was, literally talking to me about things that they noticed, there is no telling how much longer I would have gone on thinking that your mother was helping me." Archie asked Sunny what it was they had said. "I was to go to this house after I was discharged from the facility. She just told me that I was going to be able to go home and nothing more. And I was to keep my mouth shut, her words on where I was so that her degenerate son, I always thought she meant Nash, but I don't know for sure now — wouldn't find me. I thought that was an odd thing to say, but then she told me that she'd give me money to start over wherever I wanted to go. She wasn't willing to help me with finding out the truth about what had happened but kept filling my head with all these terrible things about all her sons. That none of you were any different than Nash had done to me, and without her, there is no telling what sort of things they might do to their mates. Do you think that she meant to keep you all away from your other halves?"

"The better question would be, has she done this before? Did she, at some point in your lives, keep you away from your mates when they showed up." Archie sat down hard. He was glad that there had been a chair behind him, or he might well have hurt himself badly. Belle went to make sure he was all right, but what Belle had said about other mates had him thinking. Had she done this before?

"Why?" They all turned to Beau when he asked his question. It was a good one. Why would she do that? "Most of the time, she barely acted like she liked us. Why would she care if we found our mates and moved away? I have to admit to you guys I think this takes some looking into. Not just the mates, though I hope to Christ she'd not do something like that, but her reasoning behind it. Why would she not want us to...that's it. She doesn't want us to be happy. You think?"

"If that's the first thing that pops into your head, then that's more than likely it." All of them turned to Belle when she stood there. "As much as I'm enjoying this with all you young men, I believe we need to search this house before she gets back. There is no—"

"I know where everything you need is. We've been saving things for you." The staff, one by one, were lined up behind Mother's butler, Billings. "I've been waiting for this day. All of us have since you were young men. I'm ever so glad that one of you has gotten your heads out of your ass, and—by the way, I'm leaving my employment here as of an hour ago. The things that you need are in the living room. The rest of us, all the staff, only stayed here to make sure that you were able to find what you needed, and we'll be leaving before your mother returns. Also, I'd watch out for your grandfather, too. He's a mean little fucker that would just as soon spit on you than to help you out. Father like daughter, if you know what I mean."

"Don't go." Everyone looked at Sunny. "She's probably going to be put on trial. If I were you, Archie, I'd move into this house and make it your own. Change the locks and make sure that you find yourself a good attorney to look into the death of your father. For some reason, I think she might well have murdered him for something more than...I don't even know anything about his death, but after today, I'd think really hard about how he died."

"I'm going to do it." Archie stood up. "The house is mine anyway. When Dad died...I didn't want to push Mom out, so I let her stay here. I think she's outstayed her welcome and my goodwill toward her. Billings, if you'd stay here with the rest of the staff, I'd appreciate it. Also, so you guys know, there are a lot of things that Dad left you that Mom didn't turn over to you. I'll figure that out, too."

When they all went to the living room, Billings and the other members of the staff decided to stay. They were still going over some of the things that were in the room when the caterers arrived. Nash didn't think that this day could have gotten any stranger, but he was beginning to think that this wasn't strange. His life before had been. This was normal. At least, that's what he kept telling himself it was.

Chapter 4

LouCinda couldn't figure out why her sons would be doing this to her. All she'd done was try to make their lives better and look how they treated her. Her only phone call had been to her dad to come to bail her out. If her sons didn't straighten up soon, she was going to have to get them all together and tell them how things were going to go. Even her dad told her that she was too lenient on them at times.

She had thought about reaching out to one of her other sons, but she was in no mood to put up with their whining. They would too. Telling her that they'd come, but cash was short. She kept them on a tight leash about them having money and a job, too. LouCinda wanted them to be dependent on her and not anyone else.

Then there would be the hundreds of questions

they'd ask her about what was going on about how she had ended up here in jail. Even she'd been confused about that. Couldn't a person defend their home anymore? They'd want to know who the men were that she'd been arrested with. Why? Why? Why? She just wished that they would just do what she wanted them to and believe she was right all the time.

Nashville was nearly had to that point. Jameson too. Just a few more tweaks to their anger, and she'd have them right where she wanted them to be. The others would fall into place after that. It was the only emotion that she knew how to use against others. Love, or even loving someone, had never been something that she was good at. But her dad. She loved him more than anyone in the entire world.

LouCinda was told that she had a visitor. She hoped that she'd not have to spend the night in the cell, but almost as soon as she was chained and seated in the little room she'd been led to, her dad told her that she didn't have an amount of bail set because she'd have to wait on the judge to give her one before she could get out. Just one more thing to use against her, she thought.

"That's ridiculous. Why am I even here in

the first place?" Her dad told her what the officer had told her when she'd been brought in. "It's not kidnapping. I was only detaining them until I got what I wanted. Why does that girl care anyway? I've gone out of my way to make sure that she lived. Did you tell them that she died like I told you to do? That was an excellent plan to keep them pissed off at Nashville. Thank you, Dad."

"No troubles there, child. And I did, making sure they could see that I was pissed off about it too. I bet had Nashville been standing here with me, any one of them brothers of his would have killed him right off." Shaking his head, her dad looked at her. "They've gotten out of hand. The lot of them need to have their asses beaten. I don't know how you'd go about that with them being bigger than you are, but that's what they need."

"I shouldn't have had any kids with Archibald in the first place. I didn't want to be his mate, but once he declared me, I knew you couldn't do anything about it." LouCinda had hated her mate with so much passion that even having sex with him couldn't cool her temper. "So I'll be here until tomorrow, I guess."

"A bit longer than that, I'm afraid. Judge doesn't show up until Thursday." She had to think what day of the week this was and was not happy that she had to wait five days for someone to be able to bail her out. "I know. Don't think I didn't pitch a bitch about that too. To think that this town doesn't have the money, the mayor told me to have a full-time judge around for special things like this is beyond stupid."

Her dad had been an attorney once. Then, just after she'd married Archibald, he'd been found guilty of having sex for reduced sentences with a bunch of inmates. He was also found to be selling drugs as well as a plethora of other things that she just didn't know why anyone cared. It wasn't as if the inmates were real people, for Christ's sake. Her dad had spent the next twenty years in prison, and she had gone to see him every day to just be near him. Her dad was all the family that she considered her own.

They spoke for only a few minutes more before her time with him was up. Again, she didn't understand the rules of this place. It wasn't as if there was anyone else in the cells but the men that she'd hired to do her dirty work. They'd better keep their mouths shut, too, if they knew what was good for them.

After being taken back to her cell, she was given a menu. After looking it over twice, she asked if she could have wine instead of the offers that were on the list for beverages. After being told no, she would eat and drink what was offered or nothing at all, LouCinda, settled on a baked, not deep fried like the menu said, piece of sole as well as a salad. After crossing out the things that she wanted to be changed, like the baked instead of the deep fried sole, as well as just having a salad rather than potato salad, she handed it back to the policewoman.

"I already told you that this is what you're going to get." LouCinda told her that she didn't want all those fatty things with her meal. Also, she was ordering from the menu but only modified a few things that she wanted. "You'll get what you marked without the changes. You didn't mark what you wanted to drink."

"Wine." She just stood there. "It's not like I'm going to a nice restaurant where I might drive myself home and have an accident. Just have them slip me a glass or two of wine with my meal, and nobody will be upset. Now, go away. I have thinking to do."

When the girl left her just as she wanted, LouCinda lay on the nasty cot and thought about her boys. She'd been planning their entire life what to do if a mate showed up for them. Her first plan had been just to kill them off. But that could and more than likely would come back to bite her in the ass. Someone somewhere would miss the twit, and then she'd be in trouble. With Peter, it had been as easy as if she had planned the entire thing out herself.

They'd been taking care of women together for years, the two of them. When she'd figured out that Sunshine was Nashville's mate, the idiot had come running to her after he'd figured it out—it had been a simple thing to have Peter kill her off. While she still wasn't sure how that plan had failed by having Peter kill the woman, it still boggled her mind that he'd nearly gotten caught by Nashville.

Her plan, too, had been to find the girl and do the killing herself. Finding out that she'd hidden in a dumpster had been a stroke of luck that she'd not counted on. And LouCinda might well have been able to kill the twit off, but she had been followed into the empty building where Sunshine was by an off-duty cop, or that would have been the end of her and her making LouCinda a grandma.

Even having her sons as old as they were had been hard for her to play down the fact that her oldest was nearly thirty-four. But she'd been caring for herself, and her looks long enough to know how to keep her age from showing. It was difficult at times, but she'd managed it so far. Until Sunshine came around.

Keeping her sons from mating with their would-be mates had been her priority since each one of them had come out with a pecker instead of a pussy. A female child would have only needed a little magic to think that her appendix was bothering her and greasing a few palms and poof, no grandchildren. Men were more difficult. Cutting them to be sterile took a great deal more effort, more than she had the time for. Plus, her husband had insisted that he take them to the doctor when she'd tried that avenue. That's why he was gone. He'd stuck his nose into too many plots she had going on. The dirty bastard.

When her meal came, she was so pissed off that she nearly tossed it out of her cell. Who had potato salad with fish? Maybe deep-fried fish, like she got, but there wasn't any way that anyone with taste would eat such greasy, heavy food for lunch. She couldn't imagine what sort of food she'd get as her dinner. Once she was out of here, she was going to get the current mayor out of office so that changes would be done quickly and the way that she wanted them.

It wasn't as if she was wanting to run everything. It's just when things messed with her plans that she had to put things to right. Her priority had been to make sure that her sons did what she wanted them to do. And in a reasonable time frame. Keeping them apart by making sure that they hated each other also made it so that she could manipulate them into doing things she wanted done.

LouCinda knew that if people found out how she'd been treating her sons, especially when they were younger, she would have lost them. Or Archibald would have made sure that she wasn't around them anymore. He wouldn't have killed her. No, that wasn't his style. But he would have made her life a living hell while he was at it.

Killing him hadn't been as easy as she thought it would have. Poison hadn't done much to the bastard. Even giving him large doses like she had had only made him cautious around her. The last few years of their lives together had him going out for every meal and not even drinking a bottle of water from the household unless he tested it thoroughly against holes and such.

"Fucker." After peeling off the breading from the fish, she ended up only eating about three bites. It wasn't fit to eat either way, but without the breading to hide some of the fish taste, it was positively vile. She did end up eating the potato salad as there was nothing else but a slice of white bread — something that she wouldn't eat if she were starving, as well as a cup of coffee. Or tar. LouCinda hadn't been able to figure it out. A new menu came with her lunch, so she looked it over to see what she could get. Nothing, as it turned out. Nothing on the list that she was forced to pick from was anything that she'd dirty a plastic fork with.

"*Mother.*" Smiling, she decided to ignore her oldest son in favor of making in wait on her. She might as well start their training over while in here. "*All right, I'll speak then. I wanted to let you know that I've decided to live in the house that Father left me. Also, while I was gathering up your things out of the master suite, I found the other stipulations that were in his will and making sure that my brothers get what they were supposed to.*"

"*You will not. That's my house.*" Archie told her that it wasn't actually his but had been left to him. He'd only been allowing her to live there until now. "*You'll continue letting me live there too, until I say differently. What right do you have in being in my bedroom anyway? None, that's what rights you have on anything pertaining to me as your mother. Nor will you have any rights at all if you mess with my plans."*

"Not that it matters one way or the other what you want, Mother. It's done. I'm having the rooms cleaned from top to bottom now. You'll need to find yourself other accommodations." She asked what his brothers thought about him throwing their mother out on the streets. *"Who do you think helped me get all the furniture out of the place? It was them. We've been talking about a great many things that have to do with you and your way of making us hate each other. Did you kill our mates, mother? Mine? Or the others?"*

"No, mores the pity. I've not had the opportunity to get to any other than Nashville's. And she'll be gone quick — she's nothing but a waitress, Archie. Not a woman I would associate with our family name. And being as low life as she is, there is no telling how many brats she'd pop out that would be calling me grandma." She shivered at that thought. *"No, not yet. And see that I don't have the things back the way I want them when I get out of here, too. You might want to think about that when you're going through my drawers at my home."*

LouCinda was happy that Archie didn't have anything to say to her again after that, which satisfied her to no end. LouCinda was going to have to get her dad to help her out while she was stuck in here. The boys needed to have their asses beaten just like he'd said. And he'd do it, too. Her dad would do anything for her.

When they came to get her dinner menu, she told them that she wanted to order out and have it brought to her. There were rules about that, too, that she soon discovered. And the ones that pissed her off the most were that there would be no acholic drinks, no steak knives, and nothing that had to be kept cold or hot as they didn't have the manpower to bring her different dishes when she was ready for it.

"What do you expect me to order then? A pizza? No way in hell am I going to eat a pizza, one of those nasty-looking pies, when I should be able to have as much steak as I want. Damn it, I want you to call the mayor and tell him that I'm here and want to speak to him." The cop told her that he'd left word that he didn't want to speak to her, and he was happy that she was locked up. "Well, I never. You tell him that I'm not happy. I'm very unhappy, as a matter of fact. You tell him that LouCinda Sheppard is going to come after him if he doesn't do what I tell him."

The girl only told her that if she decided that

she still wanted to have a meal brought to her, just yell. Like she was some kind of fisherman's wife, who would stand out on the front porch and make loud grunting noises or something. She reached out to the only person that would understand her.

"Dad. I'm so upset right now. I want to have a decent meal, and they're not letting me. Also, and this one I've already taken care of, Archie was moving me out of my house. Can you believe that? Like he has some balls to do that to me. I told him that he'd better not...why aren't you answering me?" He told her that she'd not given him a chance. *"Well, I am now. What are you going to do about this? I'm mad that I can't do it myself, being locked behind these doors."*

"Just give me a minute now, and I'll drive by the house. I had a doctor's appointment today, and I couldn't get any of those boys to take me there either. Of course, they all had good excuses, but I hate to drive when I don't have to." LouCinda asked him why he'd gone to the doctor. *"Never you mind about my problems. You just keep yourself out of trouble there and get home."* When he paused for a little bit, LouCinda tried hard not to rush him into telling her what was going on. *"Darling, you're not going to believe it. Not only is there a couple of big semi's in front of your house, but it looks like there*

are crews all over the place doing painting and trimming trees. Oh my. Your boys are all together, too. Plotting, no doubt. Want me to take care of this?"

"Yes. My goodness, Dad, they're going to have their heads rolled if they keep this up. Archie said that his brothers were helping him move my things out. There is no telling what they're saying about me to each other. Is that girl there too?" Dad told her that she was. *"This isn't going to go well for any of them, especially for Nashville and that twit. I'm going to need to get out of here sooner rather than later now that this is going on. See what you can do about that for me, too."*

"I'm going to talk to the boys. They'll see reason before I get back to you on what they're doing." She felt his anger and wondered what had happened to her dad. *"They've moved my things out too. Damn it, this means war. See that I don't shed some of their blood for this. I'm going to have to get in touch with the leap leader, too. This is no way to treat their mother."*

This would not bode well for any of them if she had to get pissed off at them more so than she was right now. Damn it. She'd only been in jail for less than twenty-four hours, and they were acting like they had all kinds of rights to do things. LouCinda felt her head aching again and laid down. The doctor told her that she needed to have less stress in her life, and here her boys were making her sick again. Well, she'd be out soon, and she'd show them. See that she didn't.

~*~

Nash watched his grandfather walking up to the front steps to the house. The locks had been changed about an hour ago, and he was happy about that. Also, the police were on standby to make sure that people didn't get in the house unless they approved them. That only included their mother and grandfather, but it was enough. When he got close enough to them, he drew back his fist to hit one of them. It just happened to be Sunny, that he aimed his meanness at.

"Touch her, and I'll kill you." Sunny moved out of his reach when Archie grabbed his grandfather's hand before he was able to release it. "What do you want? Whatever it is, I'm not interested."

"You put that stuff back in the house, or so help me, Archie, I will take you on. This house don't belong to you." Archie shoved a copy of the will. He had several more copies to hand out to people who asked him what he was doing. "This don't mean shit. Your momma has been staying there since her husband passed on. You didn't say shit then. Put it

all back, and I won't have to call the cops on you all."
Grandfather looked at all of them, then at Sunny.
"You should be ashamed of yourself for treating
your mother like you have been. First, you go against
her wishes, and then you have her arrested — in her
own home. You all are going to pay for this."

"I'm not worried about what you do anymore.
I have to admit I'm ashamed of myself and my
behavior on how I've been told to treat my brothers
and new sister. But no more. And I found the money
too. It's amazing to me that our own mother would…
well, it's water under the bridge, as Dad used to say.
Did you kill him, Grandfather? Had you anything
to do with his death?" Grandfather asked him what
he was talking about. "It's just a question. I've
spoken to a good attorney, too, one that works for
us, not Mother and you, and he is working on getting
Dad's body exhumed. I don't think that I'm going
to have any trouble getting someone to do that for
us. Doesn't seem like you nor mother are very liked
around town."

If he'd not been looking directly at their
grandfather, he might well have missed the look of
fear. When he swayed slightly, paling a little as he
did, not one of them reached out to steady him. Nash

thought that was very telling.

"You boys are going to cause more trouble than your asses can cover if you don't stop what you're doing right now and go back to listening to your momma." It was Jameson who said they thought they'd lived longer if they didn't listen to either of them. "You ungrateful cur. You just wait. Your momma is going to be getting out of that cell she's in, and—why haven't any of you gone there to see her? You need to get your asses down there and be sucking up to her. Don't you love her anymore?"

Nash was shocked that the word 'no' slipped out of his mouth before he could think how it sounded. But he didn't worry all that much. The others, all six including Sunny, said that they didn't like her either. Weston went as far as to tell Grandfather that they didn't much care for him either.

If he was pissed off, he didn't show it for very long. As soon as it was apparent that none of them were going to do what he wanted, Grandfather turned on his heel and left them there, pulling out his cell phone as he left the property. Nash looked at his brother when he said his name.

"Thank you." Nash asked him what he was thanking him for. "For not holding a grudge against us. Especially me. Thank you for standing up to Mom when you did. And more than anything, I want to thank you for just being there for me. You have been, too. For all of us in making sure we are getting the information that we need to make this work. Legally too. Thank you for that."

Nash wasn't sure what to say to his brother, so he did something that he'd not done with any of his family in decades. He pulled him to him for a hug. A great bear of a hug that he thought he needed more than his brother did. After a few seconds, the six of them were hugging in a group hug. Nash felt tears fill his eyes when he thought of the warmth that he was feeling for the first time in longer than he could remember. That was when it occurred to him that he'd not had a hug from either his grandfather or mother since he could remember.

Letting that thought slide away, he hugged Sunny, completely forgetting that she had a no-touch rule going on right now. Not that he blamed her. However, just as he was stepping back to allow her breathing room, she called it, the others hugged her, too. One at a time, they pulled Sunny to them and hugged her tightly while welcoming her to the family.

Nash was happy with the way things were going. He hoped it stayed that way, them being close. At least trying to be close. While he wasn't sure when it all started that they were shoving each other away, he knew now that it was their mother and grandfather. Why they'd do that wasn't anything that he knew, but he wasn't going to allow either of them to do this to him again. He only hoped that he was brave enough to stand up to her more often.

Looking at Sunny while she helped with the furniture being moved, he knew that she was going to be a huge part of them getting their feet back under them. He knew, too, that without her at his side, there was no telling how much longer he would have gone on hating everything and everyone.

The last several pieces of furniture were out of the house and being loaded onto the trucks when he realized that they'd skipped lunch. Asking Sunny if she wanted to get dinner with him, she agreed but asked if he wanted to invite his brothers. Nodding, she smiled at him. Nash would have given her just about anything for her to look at him like that again. Turning away, he asked his brothers if they wanted to join them for dinner. Their agreeing had his heart fill up so full that he had to stand still for several seconds to get his heart beating again.

"I'll meet you all there. I have a couple of things that I need to take care of before we eat." Nash asked Archie if he could help him. "Nah, I got this. Also, you'll all be happy to know that I just heard from the man we hired to represent us about Dad's death, and he said that the judge is more than willing to help us out by having Dad's body exhumed and an autopsy done on him. So that's good."

Nash didn't think it was going to be good information to come out about their father's death. He didn't know why, but he had a feeling that Grandma should be exhumed, too, along with several people who had died suddenly after having a run-in with their mother. He didn't say anything as he and Sunny made their way to his truck, however. He was concerned enough as it was, and he knew that voicing his concerns with her wouldn't help. She'd be giving him her own list of people who needed to have their deaths looked into deeper. It made him smile when he thought of how she'd gone toe to toe with Archie when he said that he didn't want their mother to die in prison.

"Oh, so you want her to be able to stew about how you've all gotten balls, and when she is let out, she'll take them back from you. Harshly too. Is that what you want, Archie? Because if you ask me, that's likely going to come back on you, all of you, if she's released to go back to the way things were." Archie looked at him for just a second until Sunny jerked his head back around to her. "I'm the one speaking to you right now. Your brother knows that I'm right. She'll come back here, and if I don't miss my bet, kill the lot of you like I'm sure she did her husband and mother, and then I'm dead too."

"You think she killed my dad?" Sunny asked him what he thought after finding all the things that he had in her bedroom. "I guess I don't want to believe that she'd be that heartless. All right. We'll have Dad exhumed. Then, the others from there. Does that make you feel better? And I'm serious too about making you feel better, Sunny. You're scary when you're right."

"I'm not right nearly as often as I wish I was, but in this, I believe that I am. She's got it in her head that she has to control you guys. Why? Who knows for sure, but she won't just let that go simply because you've decided you've had enough. LouCinda is dangerous. And so is your grandfather."

Throughout the rest of the afternoon, while

moving furniture out, each of his brothers went to Sunny to get advice about things that Mother had done to them. He was surprised, too, to find out that their mother pitted them against each other since they were just boys. A lot of things were falling into place since he'd woke up—what he was calling not being so angry all the time. But mostly, it was finding Sunny to be a part of his life.

Staggering a little, he held onto the truck before getting in. Nash realized something just then that had him nearly falling over. He loved his mate. He was so in love with Sunny that he felt the feeling wash over his entire body.

"Are you all right?" He nodded, then shook his head. "Well, that's about as clear as mud. Are you going to get in, or do you want me to drive? I don't know how. I've never been able to afford a car, but I'm sure it's not that hard. I mean, if you can do it, I can too, right?"

"I love you." She stared at him with a cocked brow. "I'm sorry. That didn't come out right. Not that I don't love you, I do. But I should have…I don't know, lead up to it better?"

"I don't know what to say to you about that." He nodded and reached for the door handle. "I think

I'm falling in love with you too, Nash. But as I've never had this feeling for anyone but my grandma, I don't know how I feel. Can you give me time?"

"All the time in the world." Getting into the truck after opening the door for her, he nearly did a jig on the way to his side. Christ, he was in love, and it felt really good. He was going to make it up to her for the rest of their lives on how he'd treated her at the beginning of their relationship. Yes, he thought, he had a lot of making up to do and thought he was going to enjoy every second of it.

Chapter 5

Sunny watched the brothers talking to each other. And they were actually enjoying themselves. She had a feeling that they'd not done this unless it had been harsh words since they were children. The six of them seemed to be just getting to know one another. That was, she thought, one of the saddest things she'd ever witnessed.

"I have some things that I found at the house. I mean, I knew it was there but didn't find it until I located the safe. Mother had hidden it away since she'd had no way of unlocking it without my permission." Archie handed each of them an envelope. "I hadn't any idea until I got the safe opened that she'd never...it doesn't matter now, I guess. I can give it to you now. It's part of your inheritance from Dad. And when I say part, there is more coming each of your way. Dad, despite being married to Mother, was a good businessman. And he made sure that we would all be taken care of when he was gone."

Nash opened his envelope, looked briefly inside, and then handed it to her. She wasn't sure why he'd want her to know what he'd gotten, but she looked inside the envelope too. Closing it quickly, she tried to hand it back to Nash, but he wasn't having it. Lying it on the table between them, she had to make herself sit still. She tried her best to pay attention to what was being said, but all she could think about was how many zeros were on the five checks that were stashed in the thing.

"There is also a plot of land that I didn't know about for each of you to do with as you please. It's part of the land that the house sits on. Hundreds of acres that I'm sure that mother didn't know about either since, again, she couldn't get the safe open." Wrangler asked how she'd gotten away with keeping this from them. "I don't know. As I said, I didn't know about the deeds, or I would have said something a lot sooner. The money? To be honest with you, I didn't know that you'd not received that as yet. I, as I know the rest of you were, was devasted when Dad died, and I couldn't think beyond him being gone. I think now that I can look back on it, I think that Dad kept Mother under control as best he could. I don't know about you guys, but I'm seeing things from the past that I didn't before. Whether it was because I just didn't see it or I didn't want to, but I think this thing she was doing to us has been going on for a long time."

"She wanted us not to have mates. Not to mention wanting us to be totally dependent on her for everything. Including money." Archie nodded and sat down when Nash spoke. "She was…I have a feeling that she meant for Sunny to die the day that she found out what she was to me. And if I'd not come up on Peter when he knocked her down, he would have killed her. I think that we need to look into things deeper about what else they might have done to other women around town."

"I've given a list of missing women to my grandma. It wasn't my list; the place where I worked had it. Grandma has someone looking into it now." Archie thanked her. "You're welcome. You should also know that Grandma is looking into other deaths around the town, too. Missing women and children. I'm not saying that your mother had anything to do with their missing, but I also think she might well be guilty of a lot of things that have been happening, too."

"I agree with you, Sunny." Beau stood up. She liked this brother a little more than she did the others. He was calming and quiet. But she also knew that someplace below the surface sat a beast that no one would survive from if he ever unleashed on you. "I don't know about the rest of you, but I've been working without her knowledge. I know that Mother would have had a fit—well, more than a fit if she'd known about that but I didn't like not being able to have any money on me unless she approved it. I have invested well, better than I thought that I could, and have amassed a fortune for myself. Millions and millions of dollars, as a matter of fact. So if you, any of you, need some money, I will gladly turn over as much as you need."

Nash laughed. "I've done the same thing. In addition to working from home, I've also managed to put away a bit of money on my own. Like you, I didn't want to be beholden to anyone for some extra cash. In fact, now that I think about it, I think Dad sort of hinted that I keep my work separated from Mother. He said that she didn't need to know everything."

The others said that they'd been doing the same. In fact, Jameson was an attorney just waiting for the change to put out there that he was taking on clinics. All of them said it was their dad who had told them the same thing he'd told Nash. And it occurred to her then that these men were all worth more money than she'd ever seen in her life. Sunny began to tense up, and it was then that Nash took her hand again.

"Don't. Don't think that." She stared at him. "We've bonded, love. I can feel your every emotion. I can look if I wish, but tell me why you're all the sudden afraid to sit here with us."

"I don't belong here." He picked up her hand and kissed the back of it. "You're all...Nash, I'm just a waitress in a restaurant that barely sees the kind of money that you're talking about in years. If ever. You need to find yourself a deb or something."

"I have found the woman that has completed me in you. You might not be aware of it yet, but you saved us. All of us. Had you not come along when you did, I might well have...to be honest, I don't know what I might have done had you not come along when you did. I'm not angry anymore all the time. And when I find myself starting down that road again, I just have to think of you, and I feel so much better. I've noticed, too, that my brothers are going to you when they need answers. How Archie has accepted me back without question. All of my brothers have, and I find that more enjoyable than I ever thought possible. Thank you for giving my family back to me. You've pointed out things to us, some you might not even be aware of, that you've done for us that made us realize that things weren't as good as we thought they were with our mother. We were blinded by…anger is the only thing that I can think of. She blinded us to what she was doing to us by our own anger. And we might even find out that she's killed our father. Or had him killed. Those are things that we would never have pursued had you not come into our lives."

"I just was an outsider that pointed out a couple of things." He told her that a set of new eyes made the difference. "You're making me out to be some kind of all-seeing person. I'm far from that, Nash."

"And I'm looking forward to getting to know everything about you, love." He kissed her on the cheek and then smiled at her. "I'm so sorry that you were hurt not just by me but also by my mother. But I'm going to make it up to you. Every day for the rest of our lives."

She didn't want that and told him so. "I just want things to be normal. Do you think that's possible?" He shook his head no at her, then laughed, drawing the attention of the rest of the people at the table. After waving them off, she picked up her new cell phone when it rang. It had been a gift from her grandma. That's who was calling her now.

"I have good news and bad. Which do you want first? All though, I'm thinking that it might well be all good news once you share with that new family of yours." She asked if she could put her on speakerphone so that everyone could hear. "Yes. Brilliant idea. Yes, honey, do that so I can tell you all."

It took her a few tries to get the phone to work, hanging up on her once. But simply handing the phone over to Nash, he had it set up in no time. Grandma was laughing when Sunny told her who was at the table with them.

"Hello, my dear boys. I have adopted you all to my heart, just so you know. My kittens. Thank you. All right. News. I'm not going to qualify it and let you each decide if it's good or bad. All right?" They all agreed. "Your grandfather has been arrested. Oh my, he does have a potty mouth on him, doesn't he?

When the body was being exhumed of your father, he went there to stop it. I don't know the man, but there was an off-duty FBI agent there who was hanging out with his cousin at the site when it happened. Your grandfather hit the agent when he told him that he was going to be arrested if he didn't back off. Hitting a federal officer, on or off duty, is a big no-no." No one moved for a few seconds until Archie started laughing. The others joined in. "Good for you guys. That's the spirit. I've also heard that your mother is causing trouble at the jail. Wanting…well, demanding things is more what she's doing. Special treatment as well as special foods. The jail gives you a menu, and your mother thinks that if she just writes what she wants on it, it'll happen. It's not by the way. The police have been just blowing her off, which is making her more upset. Okay, the other news. The men that were arrested with your mother have been given a deal. If they rat her out, they'll receive a lighter sentence. None of them had a permit to carry their weapons, apparently. I, for one, am glad that this is going to be coming back on her. Especially if those men tell the Feds anything incriminating against the two of them — meaning your grandfather and mother. Those men have apparently worked for your mother for the last fifteen years. That's a long time as being the hitmen for her."

"You think they'll talk?" Grandma told Wrangler that she didn't see any reason why they wouldn't. "Yes, maybe. But she has a way of getting what she wants no matter what it is. I just worry that's all."

"I'm sorry that you all had to go through all that. I truly am. I'd legally adopt you all if I could. I just love that my little granddaughter is so happy now." Sunny flushed when Nash smiled at her. "All right then. As soon as I get news, I'll get it to you. Oh, this is the most fun I've had in a long time. Before I forget. I've checked on things. My license is still standing, so I can represent you when this goes to trial. And I'm going to make sure that it does. While I was checking in my licenses, I found that Jameson is also a licensed attorney. If you'd allow it, young man, I'd love to have you second chair me. You can't first, of course, not with it being your family, but we'll work around that, you and me. If you'd like?"

"Yes, I'd be honored to do that. And if I could have a bit of yours and Sunny's blood—all of our blood, actually, we'd be better at communicating all the time. With Archie's permission, of course."

Archie, being the oldest, agreed wholeheartedly to them exchanging blood. "It might keep us all a bit safer too."

"Mrs. Nettles, why don't you join us here at the restaurant. We've only just ordered. Perhaps you can join us for dessert." Beau told her where they were. "You've done so much for us; the least we can do is pay for you a piece of pie for all your help."

In the end, Grandma did join them for dessert. She'd always been a big pie person and wasn't ashamed to order two slices since she'd missed dinner with them. As they were leaving after paying the bill, Archie decided he was going to sleep in the big house tonight. She and Nash went to his apartment and sat on the mattress. Before she could realize just how exhausted she was, Sunny laid back on the temporary bed and closed her eyes. It was just what she needed to get some shuteye. A soft mattress and someone to watch over her.

Waking sometime in the darkest part of the night, she felt someone behind her. It took her a few minutes to remember that it was Nash, and she moved closer to him as he spooned against her. Closing her eyes, she wondered if this was what it would be like in their life together. Sleeping like this, cuddled close to each other. It was a feeling that she thought that she could really get used to.

"We need to go to the store and get some things for us to be able to live with until we can find us a house. I don't know about you, but I already don't like sleeping on an air mattress." She loved that he whispered to her, and she did the same thing back to him in saying that a bed would be nice. "I agree with you there. I have a house. It's not that big, two bedrooms. It's a rental that I was renting out until recently. Also, this complex is something that I own as well. I have a lot of properties around the area that I've been buying on the sly for some time now. I want to build us a forever home on the land that my dad left me if you want that, too. Also, I don't know how you feel about children, but I would like some with you. What do you think?"

"I would love to have your child or two." He hugged her from behind. "I've only ever lived in an apartment. Even my parents didn't own a house. Grandma and Grandda owned a house. I would go stay with them through the summer months. I miss my grandda."

"If you don't mind me asking, why didn't you ever get help from your grandma when you were barely making it? I know that it's none of my business, but I was just curious." She told him everything. "I can understand you being embarrassed about being in the situation that you were in. It makes me feel better that she didn't refuse to help you other than you just not asking her. You won't have to worry about money again, love. I promise you that we're going to be just fine."

"I hope so. And the sooner we can get this settled with your mother and grandfather, the better I'll feel, too." She lay there for several minutes, thinking about the things that LouCinda had said to her while she was getting better. She wasn't going to tell Nash tonight, but she had a feeling that he should know soon enough, especially about LouCinda telling her that Nash was worthless and that he'd never amount to anything. She wondered what the woman was going to say when she figured out that her boys, despite having her as a mother, did all right for themselves.

~*~

Their first stop to shop had ended in disaster. Not for them, but...Nash still laughed when he thought about the man's look on his face when he realized that he and Sunny were there to buy some furniture regardless of what his mother had said about him. Apparently, his mother had given strict rules to a lot of department stores about her boys not having a pot to piss in, and if they sold them anything, then she wasn't going to pay them for it.

After a quick call to the bank by the store manager, they were falling all over themselves to wait on them. But Sunny had that look in her eye that meant that things were not going to be easy for the store. She put her arms over her chest and tapped her foot. Nash thought for sure that the manager would have had her baby for her had she only said the word.

"You treated us like dirt when you found out what our last name was, and now you figure since we have money in the bank out the ass, you can suddenly wait on us. Well, I, for one, wouldn't buy a stick from this place if it was the last place on the earth to buy one. You could have asked us, and we would have provided you with…no, you had to turn your nose up at us and act as if we were somehow less than people." The manager said that they'd been given orders. "Orders from who? Your boss? Because that's the only person that I would think you'd be taking orders from. As a matter of fact, I'd like to speak to your boss. I'm sure he'll have plenty to say after I'm finished with him."

Not only did she chew out the manager's boss, but she also told them that they were thinking about buying the place from them just to put them out of work. He was impressed by the thought, but he knew that if he did that, Sunny would murder him. By the time they were leaving, the customers there had heard how they'd been treated, and most of the people there were returning their purchases or leaving altogether. Nash was going to put Sunny in charge of calling people when their rent was due. She'd be damned good at it.

This was their third store and the second time they'd been refused service. He didn't like it, but they did get out of there faster after talking to the owner of the place. Not only did they get the things that they had wanted, but they were being delivered today, set up, and at a fat discount. Yes, Nash thought, she was going to be in charge of every bill collection that he had. Perhaps he'd get his brothers to hire her.

"The only thing that we don't have is linens. I don't know a great deal about buying towels, but I do know that I don't care for silk sheets." She asked him why. "They're slippery when you're moving around on them. When I make love to you on a bed, I want to be able to keep you on me or beneath me without having to slide you around to do it."

She stared at him for five full minutes, he'd bet, before she turned on her heel and left him standing there. He found her in the kitchen department looking at plates. When he touched his hand to her shoulder, she didn't bother turning but spoke to him the way she was standing.

"The only time that I've had sex was with you. I enjoyed it to a point, but I was hurting in my head and heart, so I didn't know what to do. I still don't. I'm assuming you've had practice." He told her that he had, yes. Not mentioning the fact that he'd made love with a woman just before meeting her. "Can you not bring them up when making love to me? I don't know if I could handle that or not. If you compared me to them. I'm a novice, as I said, so that would devastate me if I were to disappoint you any."

Turning her around to face him, he could see the streaks where her tears had fallen. Wiping them away as gently as he could, it hurt him that he'd done this to her. That he'd made her cry by joking around at her expense.

"You're the only woman for me from now on,

Sunny. I swear to you that I will never even look at another woman. I'm sorry that I made you cry." She told him that she didn't want to disappoint him. "You could never do that. Ever. Even if we never made love, I couldn't be disappointed in you for anything. I love you. And I'm going to say that to you for the rest of our lives."

Holding her, he was glad now that no one had come with them shopping. It was fun but very stressful, too. But these little things that he was learning from her about both of them were something that he didn't want to share, just with her.

Linens turned out to be easy enough to buy. Glad to be able to look up just what they were going to need in the way of towels, sheets, and other items that flushed out their home had helped them a great deal. Just as it was coming up on dinner time, they decided to finish up the evening by looking at things that would decorate rather than the functional things they needed. He had a wonderful time just picking out the little things that would sit around the house that said that he and Sunny had picked them out. After that, they headed to dinner.

Just as they were being seated, someone came up from behind him and poked him several times in his back. He wanted to ignore the person, but they were persistent, and he finally turned to look at the woman. If he knew her name at one time, he didn't now, and he tried smiling at her when she called him Nashville. She could only be a friend of his mother's, was all he could think about.

"Yes, may I help you?" She asked him if he knew where his mother was. "May I ask what this is concerning?"

"You being out on a date is what this is concerning. Does your mother know what you're doing? Or have you picked this woman up on the street corner? The last time I spoke to your dear mother, she told me that she had to keep you, of all her sons, on a tight leash before you knocked up someone, and she was—" the woman shuddered. "Before you made her a grandma. Women of our stature and age do not need little ones around to remind us that we're not getting any younger."

"No, I can see that you're much older than I thought when I first looked at you." He nearly burst out laughing when the woman gasped. He turned to Sunny and winked at her, knowing full well that she had to have heard every word she had said about her. "This is my hooker for tonight. You're not going to believe this, but she agreed to marry me if she can get my rocks off. Sunny, I'd like for you to meet..." Turning to the woman, he smiled again. "I can't remember your name, ma'am. Did you go to school with my grandda? He's in jail, too, with Mother. You should go talk to her. I'm sure she'll have plenty to say when she finds out that I'm going to get married soon." He was glad when Sunny got in on the fun.

"You know what he told me I could do? I'm going to go to his momma's fancy house and try on her pretty clothing. It'll be a little old on me, but I'll feel so fancy. And I get to wear her jewels, too." Sunny winked at the other woman as she leaned in with a slightly elevated whisper. "I'm going to give Nashville here a real treat and let him fuck me with them all over my body. Don't you think that'll be kinky?"

The woman stormed away after staring at the two of them with her mouth hanging open for a bit. The two of them were still laughing when the waiter came to take their order. Nash told Sunny that he was sorry for calling her a hooker.

"It was fun. And I don't understand how she thought we'd be all right with her coming here and berating us for something that was none of her business." Nash said that it really wasn't something new for him. "I'm sorry to hear that. To not be able to just go about your personal business without people thinking they have a right to criticize you about it. Do you suppose she'll go tell your mother? I wouldn't put it past her. They seem like the same type of woman, don't you think?"

"You've no idea." When their salads came, he decided to ask Sunny what he'd been wanting to know before. "When mother was supposed to be helping you get better, can you tell me what she said to you about her sons? I guess I'm asking if she talked badly about us."

"She did." Sunny put down her fork and looked at him. "At first, I wasn't sure why she was telling me all this stuff. Then, after a couple of days of her talking about you especially, I thought that she had to have had it wrong. Or she was joking around. Even though we had started out badly, the picture she painted of you had you sound like a homicidal maniac. Seriously. That you'd been the one that killed your father off and that you made a habit of screwing whatever came your way. Male or female. Also, she said that you more than likely carried all kinds of diseases from your being promiscuous. I knew that couldn't be true, you being a shifter. Also, you have children that you don't claim. Again, I knew that couldn't be true either."

Nash was shocked at what his mother had said about him but not really too. She had wanted them to be apart, he and Sunny, and would tell whatever she thought would work to her. He was still thinking about what his mother had said when Sunny poked him in the arm.

"The police are here. They're coming this way." He turned to look at the two officers that he'd met previously around town. Even knowing them as little as he did, Nash knew that they had to have a good reason for coming to talk to him. "Gentlemen? If you've come here to tell us what is good to eat, I'm afraid that we've already ordered. Won't you join us?"

"This is an official call, I'm afraid." Nash turned when someone put their hand on his shoulder, and he was glad to see that it was Archie. His other brothers were there as well, all grabbing chairs from empty tables to have a seat with them at the table. "Mrs. Shodan called in a complaint that you were in here with…she said that you were entertaining a lady here and didn't have the money to pay. I wouldn't have bothered you at all had I known it was your mate, Nash. I'm truly sorry about this."

"Sit down." The men scrambled getting chairs when Sunny commanded them to have a seat. "You should have called him, don't you think? Or, at the very least, waited to see whether or not we weren't able to pay. That's what I would do."

Belle joined them as well. When she winked at him, he knew on some level that things were about to get bad. Worse, he supposed, would be a better term. When she waved down a waiter and asked for a larger table, the staff nearly fell over themselves accommodating her.

"It pays to have a scanner at times. What are you having, Sunny? We should order some appetizers, too. For the table." Belle looked at the two officers sitting around the table, too. "Have you eaten, young men? I know for a fact that the onion blossom is out of this world."

"We're on duty, ma'am." Belle asked them if they'd had their dinner yet. "No, ma'am. We were headed there when we got the call to come here."

"Yes, I heard that. And my granddaughter is correct. You should have made some phone calls before embarrassing everyone by showing up without all the information. I think I'll need to make a call to your boss in the morning." The older officer pulled on his collar and said that he was sorry. The younger man ordered himself a burger platter along with a shake. "Good for you, officer. You must keep up with your intake."

By the time they had all eaten and had their empty plates cleared away, the officers told them how they'd been called to come and arrest both himself and Sunny. Now that they had a better handle on what was really going on, the two men enjoyed the meal with them and even allowed them to pay for their dinner.

Nash asked them how they'd ended up coming here when Belle told him. "I heard it on the scanner that there was trouble here. Since I knew you two were shopping, I figured that you were having dinner, and it could only be the two of you. So I called your brother, Archie, and let him know and asked him to come here too." She put her hand over his and patted it. "I can't have my future grandson-in-law getting into trouble before the big day, now can I? When are you going to put a ring on her finger, Nash? I have one for you if you want it."

"I would love that." Right there in front of

his family, he got down on one knee to propose to Sunny. The ring, a beautiful diamond with sapphires all around it, fit her finger perfectly, and both of them were nearly giddy with happiness.

Chapter 6

The furniture was delivered while they were out. He'd never been so glad for friends than he was at that moment. Not only had they brought it all in, but it was pretty much where they had wanted it all to go, too. It was really nice to have a chair to sit in when in the kitchen, too.

There was a great deal of it, too much for the house they were staying in, but it was easy enough to store what they didn't need right away in two of the apartments that were empty right now at the complex he and now Sunny owned. As soon as the house that they decided on was finished, they'd have as much fun putting all the new things into it and settling in. Even his brothers, all of them, decided to build on their property, too.

"I'm exhausted. I don't know about you, but

I think I could sleep for a year." Sunny agreed with him, and they sat on the couch that was as soft as he was hoping their bed would be. "Tomorrow is the trial, I guess, for your mom and grandfather. What do you think will happen with it? Do you suppose they'll get jail time?"

"Christ, I don't see how they wouldn't. I don't know what they found out about the autopsies on Dad or Grandma, but it can't be good the way that the police are hanging around the grave sites all the time. I mean, just according to Jameson, it's going to be a slam dunk for the court systems." She asked him if he was going to be sorry she was jailed. "No. And like you asked me to do the other night, I've been thinking about it a lot. What would I do if she's suddenly not around all the time? Stuff like that. I've come to the conclusion that I won't miss her at all. Either one of them, as a matter of fact. I'm going to enjoy my new freedom with my wonderful mate."

They had to rest twice going up the stairs. Really, it wasn't so much resting as it was talking about this and that. The carpets had been taken up on the stairs just yesterday, and they were loving all the hardwood accents around the place. Even the walls had been taken down to the bare wood, and they loved it.

Getting into bed while Sunny changed had him dozing off and on. Mostly off. He knew that a great deal of his exhaustion had to do with just having stress taken off his shoulders. Having someone to talk to who wasn't family, too, helped him a great deal. He'd never really thought of how much stress could affect a person until now. It really was like a huge burden being lifted off his entire body.

Suddenly, he found himself on his back, and Sunny was straddled across his chest, holding his hands over his head. He didn't move, didn't even struggle against her. His body reacted immediately to her closeness, his cock hardening, his cat purring for her.

"I'm suddenly not all that tired. How about you?" Nash pretended to think about it, then kissed her. "That's what I thought. I can't stand to just sleep with you anymore, Nash. I want to feel you inside of me like before. Only this time, I want us to both enjoy it. All right?"

"Yes. Anything you want, I'm there for you." She grinned at him, and that was when he noticed that she was still dressed. "However, making love requires us to both be naked. Are you all right with that?"

Sunny was looking at him. His face was so close, and his chest mere inches from hers, that he knew all he had to do was pull gently, and she'd be covering him with her body. He wasn't sure that was what he wanted, not yet at any rate. When she moved down his frame, wanting to move off of him to the floor, the sheet shifted, and he was suddenly naked beneath her. He was hard, his excretion pressing into her softness. For long moments, neither of them moved, never said a word, and just looked into each other's eyes.

His body moved up of its own accord, moving against her soft folds again, moving along her body, the friction bringing a deep moan from her and a growl from him. When she hesitated, he stopped breathing for a moment, his breath catching in his chest. He didn't want to frighten her, but he didn't want her to stop, either. She would more than likely kill him if she did that. Slowly, he moved his hands down from hers and captured her in his, holding her by lacing his fingers into hers.

Sunny moved down onto him again and again. On the next surge of her body's downward motion, he moved up hard against her. Her back bowed as a moan deep within her escaped. She began riding him faster, harder, his movements meeting hers. Nash moved her hands to her breasts, squeezing them, showing her without words what he wanted to see her do to herself.

As she began massaging them, pulling at her nipples through the shirt she had on, she never stopped pushing against him; neither of them seemed to be able to stop. He slid his hands up her thighs, which were spread wider across him, then to her hips, gripping her tight, steadying her.

"Sunny, I want you. I need to taste of you. Please?" His voice was deep, husky with need, his canines aching now, ready for her, to taste her, to sip from her.

Her answering yes came out as a hiss of breath, hardening his cock to the point of pain. Nash put his hands just inside of her panties and ripped them from her on her next upward motion. It was by far the most erotic thing he'd ever heard. She moaned loud and long, and on her next move, he pulled them out from between her legs, baring her pussy and its heat to him.

Her cream was coating his cock now, making the slide smoother and hotter. She was close, close to coming; he could smell her, her scent and heat making him ache with his own need, and he wanted her to come now.

"Sunny, come for me. Come on my cock, baby, please come. Now." He felt her stiffen slightly, and the climax ripped through her, her body arching hard against him, coating his cock with her scent and cream. While she was still convulsing, shuttering with it, Nash shifted her slightly, pulling her up to her knees over him, and positioned his cock just inside the mouth of her core.

He knew she was no longer a virgin. As a shifter, he could smell her, he didn't want to hurt her, but he wanted to come inside of her, marking her with his cum. But Sunny had other ideas apparently, and she pulled her shirt up and over her head and slammed down onto him in the same movement, impaling herself onto his length.

Her scream of pain/pleasure was his undoing; he gripped her hips harder and flipped her onto her back, slamming his cock into her, deep, riding her as she had ridden him. He nearly stopped, coming to his senses seconds before she hooked her ankles around his hips. It brought them incredibly closer, their tight bond even tighter. Her hands dug deep into his shoulders, drawing blood with her short nails, pulling him deeper into her heat.

With his control gone, his need to make her his overwhelmed him. He nuzzled at her neck, kissing a path to her jugular, pulling the frantic pulse into his mouth, sucking.

"Please, Nash. Please. Make me yours. Now." She angled her head, exposing her throat to him, to his bite. With a quick lick of his tongue to take away most of the pain, he stuck fast and clean at her jugular.

Sunny's blood flooded his mouth, filling him with her spicy heat and essence. *Mine*, he thought, *finally mine*. He felt her climax with the first draw of his hot mouth against her skin, suckling her into him, drawing hard against her neck. This time, he went with her, spilling his seed deep into her, filling her. Her pussy tightened and milked him for every drop of his cum. He licked the small wound closed and kissed her and kept on kissing her until their bodies went lax, but not nearly sated.

~*~

Waking in the middle of the night, Sunny was terrified to find herself in bed alone. The side where Nash had been sleeping was still warm, so she knew that he couldn't have gone far. Hearing a noise, she looked up and saw him. Seeing the need in his eyes, she moaned.

Nash's eyes, they had changed to a dark gold in that second. Sunny wasn't sure why she could see so well in the darkness, but it was a wonderful sight to behold. She stared, mesmerized, while he fisted his cock, stroking up and down twice.

"See something you want, love?" He tightened his grip, moving his hand up and down. He was making her ache with need, and he had not even touched her yet. When he suddenly stopped and moved toward her, she stopped him.

"Don't stop that. Keep doing what it is you're doing for me." Her voice took on a purr; her body suddenly restless and needful again. She could feel her pussy weep for him. She wanted to touch him again. She wanted to look, to watch what he was doing to himself more.

"My cock, baby, it's my cock. Say it. Tell me what you want me to do with my cock." He continued to stroke himself, faster now. Her own body tightened, and her entire body ached with need. How could she want him again so soon, she thought, after they had just had sex, not but a few hours ago. She sat up, spilling the sheet away from her body, it pooling at her knees, baring her body for him. He moved closer to her as she reached for him. "Sunny, tell me what you want," he demanded of her in a growl.

She licked her lips, mesmerized as his eyes darkened to a deeper gold. When she touched him, running her thumb over the blood-filled head, a tiny drop of cum seeped from the end. She gathered the drop on her finger and put it in her mouth, sucking it clean, moaning with delight.

That was all the encouragement he needed because he moved closer, cupping her head and pulling her mouth up to his, kissing her, his tongue tangling with hers, dancing a dance that lovers used. She wrapped her hand around his shaft, never breaking contact from his mouth. His hardness filled her hand, his width almost too much for her smallness. She felt the velvet covering steel, thick and hard for her, just for her. Touching his mind gently, she knew what he wanted, what he needed, and she gave it all to him.

"I want your cock, Nash. I want to taste more of you, please? Please, I need to taste you." While she begged him, she was moving her mouth down his delicious body, licking, biting, and nipping at his chest and his abdomen, moving closer to what she wanted. When her tongue touched his cock for the first time, he surged into the wet heat of her mouth and began gently fucking her. She pulled him deeper still into her mouth, licking the underside of the head, forcing a groan from deep in his body.

Sunny had no experience with sex, none in pleasing a man, and she so wanted to please him this one time and make him remember her forever. She gently reached out and touched his mind again, looking for his needs and seeing what he wanted. As soon as she touched him, it felt as if his mind wrapped around her, through her. She moaned at what she found there. His thoughts and images all centered on them and what he needed and wanted. She didn't know what was going to happen tomorrow, and his mother could take over again, or the next hour she could, so Sunny wanted her last chance with him to be memorable. Sunny was going to get as many of her own memories as she could.

She ran her tongue along the length of him, touching and then gently cupping his balls, his moans vibrating through her, intensifying her pleasure. When she swirled her tongue around his head again and cupped his balls tighter, he gripped the back of her head and began pumping into her mouth none too gently now, his need to come driving him beyond reasonable control.

She wasn't sure how she knew this, but she was sure. His balls, heavy and hot, tightened closer to his body. When he tightened his fist in her hair, pulling it hard, she was afraid he wanted her to stop. There was no way that was happening, she thought and sucked harder on his cock.

"Sunny, I'm going to come. I'm so close, baby. I want you to touch yourself. Give yourself pleasure for me. I want to watch you touch yourself. I want to watch you while you give yourself a climax."

She had never done anything like that before, but the look in his eyes made her want to try for him. When she reached between her legs and stroked her clit first with one finger, then two, she moaned with his cock deep in her throat. She experimented with her fingers until she found what brought her the most pleasure and began finger fucking her pussy with wild abandonment, her moans running along his shaft longer and faster. She could feel her climax racing to completion, her body taunt and hard with the need to come. With her other hand around him, she pumped hard as she came, wanting him to join her. With a final push, he came, spurting his cum into her mouth, down her throat, hot and fast. She swallowed him, taking all of his seed into her, not missing a drop. When she flicked her tongue at the end of his cock, catching the last drop of him with her tongue, he jerked her up to his body.

Adjusting her legs around his hips, he crossed to the wall and pressed her up against it. He surged into her hard and fast. She was wet, and her cream running down her thighs, making his entry smooth as he surged into her quickly. It did not take long for them to reach their peak again. They were both so close. It took very little to have them both tumbling over the cliff of intense pleasure, not two minutes after having a mind-blowing orgasm against the wall.

Sunny woke the next time in the bed. Alone again, but she didn't have the strength just yet to see if his side of the bed was warm or not. Nash had told her that he had plenty to do, and perhaps that was where he was. Right now, she had to pee so badly that she actually thought about just wetting herself rather than trying to maneuver out of the bed anytime soon.

It was later than she thought when she was finally able to get out of bed. Almost eight in the morning. Not really that late, she supposed, but they were supposed to be at the courthouse by eight-thirty. Getting under the hot spray of water, she was able to work out the kinks that she'd only just discovered on herself when Nash knocked on the glass door to the bathroom.

"I was just coming to wake you up. I suppose it's a good thing that you're already out of bed. I don't think we would have been really late had you been all nice and snuggly in the bed waiting for me." She told him how sore she was. "Yeah, and I'll only admit this to you. I think for sure that if we have sex like that again, I'm going to be a dead cat. All my nine lives will be used up. Anyway. Archie called here. He said he wanted us to all be dressed up like we're going to a large party. I think he means suits, but he was having trouble focusing on words today, so I had to help him. Also, Jameson said that the autopsies are all completed and that he has more news for the judge."

"Grandma has been able to do some searches too." She pulled the towel around her body, and that was when she noticed that most of her wounds were all healed, but she did have some bruising. "I'm guessing that you and me having sex. That's why

I'm healing faster. Not that it matters. But back to Grandma. She has some people in high places who are helping your brother and her with this case. I hope this goes as planned, Nash. I don't want to think of her being on the loose again."

"None of us want that. But even if she somehow gets out, none of us are going back to the way things were. She isn't going to be a part of our family again. Archie and the rest of my brothers are having much too much fun in getting together and having fun to let her…she nearly ruined us all by what she was doing. That alone should be enough to get her in trouble with the shadow." She hugged him after getting dressed. "You looked fantastic. I'm going to change my tie to match the red of that suit. We'll look powerful together."

"Tell your brothers if they have a tie that is red, they should wear it. We should be a force for her to reckon with on your terms." He loved that idea, he told her. Even his brothers were all on board with it. Archie said he was going to pick them all up matching ties so that they'd look like they were together. "You are all together, Nash. For the first time in forever, the six of you are together as it should have been from the very beginning."

"I love you, Sunny." She felt it, too, and hugged him. "I need to tell you that every day, and I will until you realize that I love you so much."

"I love you too. It's been hard for me to realize it, but I do love you. With all that I am." Nash pulled her toward him and held her. "Who knew that after the way we started out, things could go so right."

"I didn't. That's for sure. And I think that the way that we did start out has made us stronger than anyone could ever have anticipated." She agreed with him. "We'd better get going. I have a feeling that things are going to be coming out all right. I have to believe that."

"I do as well." Getting into the truck, Nash talked about getting them a car. And one for her. So that she'd not be depending on him all the time. "I've never driven before. I don't even have a license, to be honest."

"We'll have to take care of that soon." She was glad that he was driving when he said that. She was terrified of learning to drive, more so because of the things that she'd heard over the years about accidents. As they were pulling up in front of the courthouse, she hugged each of her new family members and loved that they had even got one for

Nash that matched her suit dress perfectly. Things were working out well, she thought. If only today would be just as perfect.

The six of them sat in the front row. Jameson was sitting with her grandma so he could second chair with her. She was in the middle of them all; it was like she had a special protection that she hadn't realized she needed. Taking Nash's hand into hers, she was happier than she'd been in a very long time. Perhaps all her life.

"All rise." When they stood up, the five men with her and Jameson dropped to the floor on bended knee. She didn't have any idea what was going on, so she stood her ground until someone explained. It wasn't until the judge demanded her deference before she had a small inkling as to what the hell was going on.

"What the hell are you doing here? I take it you're some kind of big deal to the cats here. Well, I'm not a cat, nor do I bow to people that I have no respect for." The man, Judge Crooksville, said that as a mate to one of his cats, she would pay him homage and respect. "Not if I don't respect you, I won't. And right now, I'm debating on whether or not to slap the shit out of you. Do you have any idea what these men have been through in their entire life? With no help from you, I might add."

"I don't answer to you. Now, you'll do as you're told, or you will be punished." She hadn't any idea how she'd moved so quickly, but she found herself with her hand around the judge's throat and him risen about three feet from the seat. "What do you think you're doing to me?"

"Release them from whatever hold you have over them, or you'll be one dead fat cat." She looked at Nash when he cleared his throat. "I thought that you couldn't gain weight when you were a cat. What the fuck has happened to this guy? Lying about in the sun as his fat cat is all I can figure."

"Sunny, honey, this is our leader, Josiha Crooksville. The leader that is there for things when we need him." Still holding him, she asked Nash how much he'd helped with their mother. "None. I mean, not that I'm aware of." He looked at his brothers, and they all shook their heads. "I guess I was wrong. He isn't there for us. I know for a fact that my father went to him several times over the years before his death. Grandma too. I think that my mate is right. You are a fat, useless cat."

The other stood up, and she continued to hold

onto Crooksville. When she looked at him, he asked to be able to take a breath, and she let go of him long enough for him to take in a nice breath, then closed her fingers around his throat again.

"What do you have to say for yourself? I have an idea that you're going to do what is right by these men since you couldn't be bothered to help them out when they really needed it. Their mother is a murderer. I believe that their grandfather is as well. What do you think?" She allowed him to answer her, then she nodded and let him go. "All right then. That's why you're here. But I have news for you, fat cat. If you don't do what is right by them, I'm going to take over your position and make sure your ass never sees the light of day again."

He inhaled several times while holding onto his throat. She had cut him at some point, and she wasn't the least bit sorry for it. The man should have gotten up off his ass a long time ago and made sure that things in his shadow were correct. As it was now there—

"Did you know about this? With my mother?" She didn't watch Archie but the man who would be holding all the cards. He confessed that he'd not. That he'd neglected a great many things that should have been taken care of years ago. "Did you know that there were women killed too? That there are missing children that we can't even begin to find?"

"I've heard from someone who is going to help with that as well. He's not a part of my shadow but a human. He'd been employed by your mother and grandfather for years." Archie asked if he knew how he was being paid. "He wasn't. Not really. Your mother kidnapped his family and held them hostage so that he'd cooperate with her. He found out they were all dead a few weeks later and that they were killed by her hand, he thought. He's been keeping records of the deaths in his own way. He'll be there to testify when your mother comes here. Also, he hasn't just killed all the women as he was told. When he was committed to killing them, he would send them on their way with his own money."

"You didn't think this would be important enough to look into?" Nash snorted when he told him that he hadn't been informed until lately. "I have lived a very sheltered life, sir, and I noticed that people are coming up missing. My mate is right. You aren't good enough to serve in the position that you're in. I think she would do a better job on one day than you've done since you've been in charge."

"I would have to agree." The woman who shimmered into the room stood near where Crooksville stood. No one moved for several seconds until each of the people in the room began to fall to the floor. "Oh, do get up and act like the men that I've come to admire. Thank you, Belle, for contacting me. It's so good to see you again after all this time."

"You're very welcome. I figured after all this time of someone burying people on your lands might have found its way to you. But one of your kind, he told me that you didn't know how to go about with humans involved. Well, next time you have some trouble, Lily, you give me a shout. I'll make sure that you're well-informed. All right?"

"Of course." When the beautiful woman turned to her, she felt the others in the room move to stand beside her. "She's as safe with me as she is with anyone else in this room. On this, I swear it. Sunshine, you're as beautiful as I heard you were. My goodness, you make me weep with your beauty."

"Who are you?" The woman laughed, as did the others in the room. "I don't have it in me to be polite today. So speak your peace, then move on. I want to get this shit over with today, and you're standing around holding up progress." Sunny glanced at the judge, who was staring at Lily or whoever she was like she was a goddess.

"I'm Lily, queen of the earth. Protector of the lands and magical being that has kept the earth bountiful for more generations than there are people around." She bowed before her, and Sunny didn't know what to do. "You would make a good leader, my dear child; however, I think that Archie would do well with you and your mate at his side. His mate, when she arrives here, she will be stronger than even you are. If you can believe that."

"I don't care who takes the spot or even if there is one open. I just want that woman and her father to pay for everything that they've done to my family." She assured her that they would. "Good. Then can we please get this shit started? I have a home that I want to look into its progress, and I want to have dinner with my mate."

"As you wish, my child." Sunny didn't know what was going on but was willing to put it all aside just to get this part of the day over with. LouCinda was going to pay for what she did to her and others, and there was no time like the present.

Chapter 7

LouCinda didn't know what was going on. If asked, she'd pretend that she didn't care either, but she was pissed off. There had been an explanation as to why she'd been arrested, but the answer that she was getting didn't satisfy her one bit. To her, she should have been released days ago. Instead, she was locked up with the criminal sort, and she didn't care for her being in the hallows of jail when her sons were out running around on their own. She'd heard from no less than five people that they were acting like she didn't exist, and they were free to roam about doing what they wanted all day and night long.

Now, here she was, sitting in a holding tank, they called it, waiting. LouCinda had been brought here to stand judgment over an hour ago now, and they'd put her in a room with her father since they'd arrived. Being held like she was, chained up like some kind of monster, was pissing her off too. Not to mention not allowing her the ability to use her own make-up or to brush to at least fix her hair. But at least she was able to talk to her dad.

"You said that this was never going to come back to haunt us, Dad? Why are we suddenly in jail?" He told her what he knew. "So you get arrested because they didn't ask your permission to exhume the body of your wife, and you leave me sitting around on my thumbs waiting on word from you to figure out how I'm to get out of this place. I don't understand why you'd even care if they dug up Mom or not. She's dead, isn't she? What's the big deal?"

"Because my dear daughter, thinking that she'd never be thought of as anything other than my dead mate, I buried her with the murder weapon that I used on her. That made it so that no one would find the murder weapon just lying about the house. Silly me. I thought I'd come up with the perfect plan. I didn't think that anyone would ever care about how she died, just that she was gone. The same with your husband. I'm assuming that they didn't ask you for permission to do that, either. To dig him up from his, what we thought his final resting place."

She told him what her attorney had told her. "Ah, so just because you were married to Archibald doesn't mean that you have any rights over what happens to his body. Just his blood relatives. Figures that they don't put that one out there so people know about it. Well, I guess those little shits of yours gave them permission to dig them up. Shit's going to be hard to hide once they're out of the ground. Not to mention if they start looking into other graves that are around your property. We're going to be up the shit creek without the benefit of a paddle very soon if they continue acting like they're smart enough to do this stuff we don't want."

"I don't know what you're talking about." But she did. And it terrified her just enough that she had to think of a way to throw her dad under the preverbal bus if it came to that. It would piss him off to no end, but he was old and wouldn't be around much longer anyway. She had her entire life ahead of her and she meant to make it work for herself. Even if she had to kill one or two of her kids to have it finished. "I'm not going to prison because of my sons, Dad. I want you to think about how serious I am about that not happening to me. They're selfish little fuckers, and I wish I'd never had them. But since it's too late for that now, I'm going to make them sorrier than ever for going against anything that I want. You wait and see." She glanced at the man in uniform when he snorted at her. There was another thing that she hated about being in this situation. There was no amount of privacy at all for her to do and say what she wanted.

The officer with them hadn't spoken a word to them since they'd first brought in. She could almost forget that he was there, but he was stinking up the room they were in with his overbearing cologne. After telling her and her dad to shut up talking a couple of times when they arrived, he didn't say it again. She wondered what, if anything, could happen if they were to say something damning, like leaving the murder weapons in the caskets when they'd put them in the ground. That had cost them a lot of money in the first place. She didn't believe in paying and paying for something when a person decided on a deal. Her dad speaking brought her out of her thoughts.

"Did you ever figure out that combination to that big assed safe in your house? That was pretty shitty of Archibald, if you ask me. Taunting you with it by telling you that all the answers to all your troubles were in it after he was gone. One of the reasons that I hate that man to this day. His lying to you all the time." She said that she'd not found it, but she thought that Archie had it. "Well? Why haven't you made him tell you? I'm telling you right now, LouCinda, there is money to be had in that sucker. And you should have had it all by now. Waiting around on those damned kids of yours is costing us good money all the time. A buddy of mine said that that middle one of yours, I don't know which one, never cared really, is building himself a house out on that land I have plans for."

"He will not. I don't give a shit who it is. There will be no building of anything unless I approve it. And I'm not going to." She looked up at the cop. "You there. I want you to make a call and find out which one of my ungrateful curs thinks that just because I'm not up their asses all the time, they can go about doing what they want. Do it now so that if they are in there, and they had better be, then I can nip that in the fucking bud right today."

"It's Nash." LouCinda corrected him. "No, he said that his name is Nash. It's his home that he's having built for his new wife and him. They're planning to have children too, I guess."

"Where do you get off saying stuff like that? There is no way that he is going to try and go behind — it's that woman, isn't it? That trollop that tried to get her meat hooks into him when he found her. Well, you bet that isn't going to go any further than it has right now." LouCinda asked him about her other sons. "What the hell are they doing right now? No doubt, thinking that since I'm temporarily out of their sight they can do what they please. I'll have a few lessons to teach them when I'm out of here. What's the holdup anyway?"

"The judge is gathering up the new information that was brought to his attention this morning." She asked if there was a time limit on that sort of thing. "No. There is no time limit on murder. If they find out you've killed someone and you're already dead, they can still try you."

"That's the stupidest thing that I've ever heard. Did you hear that dad? The law can put you in prison after you're dead if they find out you killed someone. I'd say that's the way to go. Kill someone, then kill off yourself so you don't have to do any prison time. Stupid, but I guess there are dumber rules around." She was still laughing about it when another officer came to get her. "What about my dad? Aren't we allowed to get this over at the same time? I want him released too when I am."

"It would be up to the judge if the two of you decide to be tried for the same crimes that the other committed. Is that what you want?" Dad asked if they'd get the same fines if it came to that. "Yes. Same everything. Sentence, fines as well as anything else that came from the verdict. Of course, this is just a hearing to find out if there is enough to hold you over for a court appearance."

"Look who's suddenly gotten all talkative. I'd like to know that I can call on you, Dad, if it comes to that and that you'll be there for me. Us being out at the same time will allow us to get twice as much work done with them, boys." He snorted again, and she found that to be the most offensive thing that she'd ever heard. After telling him to not do it again, he just laughed. "Moron. People must not teach their children to have respect for the older generation."

"Yeah? Well, I've seen how you've taught your kids. Lady, you're a monster." Before she could lay into him about what he'd said to her, he went out the door to what she could only assume was the courtroom and decided that she'd had enough. Picking up the chains so as not to get all tangled up, she was reaching for the door handle when it suddenly pushed her back. Before she could say anything to the officer about his rudeness again, he spoke. "The judge is ready for the two of you."

She didn't know who the judge was, it only just then occurred to her. Nor did she know if this person was going to take a bribe when offered. Everyone, as far as she knew, had their price. It was just getting to that point in a reasonable time that bothered her. Not the amount, however. Once a person served their purpose for her, she'd kill them and dispose of the body. It's worked out for her for decades. There wasn't any reason in her mind to think that it wasn't going to continue to work out.

The first thing that LouCinda noticed was the fire engine red dress. It took her several more seconds to realize that it was her sons who were with the person. She didn't know what the fuck was going on, but she was going to get to the bottom of it right now. However, since she was chained up, her movements were curtailed, and she could only stumble toward the men and the woman.

"Who the hell are you? And what are you doing with my sons?" The matching ties, all of the same flaming red color, seemed to mock her in some way, and she wanted to snatch them off of their throats and strangle each of them with their neckwear. "What the blue blazes is going on in here? I demand answers."

"Well, I guess it sucks to be you." The voice. It took her much too long to understand who the woman was and that she should have been dead. "We came to make sure that you had a merry sending off when they find you guilty of all the charges against you. Your father, too. If killing off your husband wasn't bad enough, the two of you killed off your mother as well. For what reason?"

"I am not going to lower myself to speak to you." She looked at the faces of the men she'd been training and disciplining since they'd been born. "I want to know why you're here. The six of you should be doing what you've been told and staying within my reach when I need you. Where have you been hiding?" It was Nashville who laughed at her question and was the first to explain himself.

"Hiding? None of us have been hiding at all but have been walking around and making friends like a normal person does. Not that it's any of your business. Also, I've been getting to know my lovely mate too. Why, it might surprise you to know that not only does the town open its doors for us—despite what you've told them, but we're making a difference around the little burg, too. Donating things. Archie has taken out all the furniture from the house that you were living in before this and given it all away." LouCinda tried once again to leap at her second son. "You're going to have to learn that we're not going to be your whipping posts anymore, LouCinda. That's right, we've decided that you're no longer going to be called any form of mother for the rest of our lives. You don't deserve it any more than your father does being called grandfather."

"I'm going to beat the shit out of you when I'm released. We'll just see how long it takes you to heal up this time, Nashville." She looked at the others and realized one thing that she'd not noticed when watching them. Not a one of them seemed to be afraid of her. In fact, they were holding their humor in a way that had her thinking that she'd been the butt of their jokes and barbs for a time now. And that wouldn't do. "What else have the six of you been up to? No good, I'm betting. Well, that's going to change too. I liked having you under my—"

"Were you going to say thumb, LouCinda? You did at that. And since you've asked—actually

asked something of us, we've decided to tell you."
She watched Archie through a narrow slit in her
eyes. "I've become an investor. Money, stocks, and
other things. I've been doing it since I was eighteen
and making pretty good money for myself and my
future mate when she comes along. And she will
now, knowing what I know about the law and how
many you've broken." The second person to speak
without her permission was Wrangler.

"You'd not believe how good I've become at
reading the market trends. Investors from all over
the world call me up to ask my opinion on what I
might think will make them some money. I have, too,
made both them and myself a great deal, too, over
the years since I turned eighteen." He looked at his
brothers, and she could see the smirks on their faces,
too, and LouCinda was getting a head pain that was
making her sick. "All of us, no thanks to you. We
have been doing very well for ourselves. Or despite
you. I'm not sure what you might call it. Dad gave us
enough money and the land to—" Her dad, chained
up as well, lunged at her sons.

"I will not allow you to sell even an inch of that
land. That is going to me even if I have to kill each
and every one of you to get—why the hell do you

think my daughter married your father in the first place? She didn't need him as her mate, and he made her life a living hell, so, in turn, mine as well. You will not do a thing to that land, or you'll wish for death more than your father did when I was finished with him." LouCinda turned back to her sons when her father spoke. "You six should have died before you were even big enough to have been spit on the sheets."

"I've heard enough." She knew that voice that spoke behind her. Just where she'd heard it from was something that she couldn't put her finger on at the moment. Winning, because that was what it felt like when her father threatened them, was too heady of a feeling for her to concentrate on something as mundane as a voice right now. "You might not care to concentrate at all, LouCinda, but I would really like it if you were to turn around and see who is going to be the last man you ever see."

She knew then. It was that fucking leader that she could never get a handle on. Turning slowly, trying her best to show her best side, she was startled to see how old he looked. How just ran down he was now. When he backed away from her touch, she smiled at him. No place like right now to get things going in her direction, she thought with a hardy laugh.

"My goodness, Josiha Crooksville. You've not aged one bit since I've seen you last." He rolled his eyes at her, and she tried her best to ignore that for now. "What brings you here? Hopefully, my sons didn't bother you with their troubles. The six of them need some discipline now and then, and it's gotten away from me for a few days. I'll take care that they never bother you again, and then we can get this, all this stuff put behind us. What do you think?"

"LouCinda, it is with great pleasure that I sentence you with pack laws and say that for the death of your mate and the twenty-nine others that we can contribute to your murdering hand that you'll be dealt with by pack laws and not human laws." She sputtered for a few seconds, trying her best to tell him that she didn't know what he was speaking about when he continued. "Yes, I know all about your deeds. And I have proof of them as well. As of the moment that you leave this building, you'll be dealt a hand of death by your kind. A death that I hope you suffer with greatly."

"I have money." Josiha said that she didn't have anything anymore. "What do you mean? You mean what they've been saying about kicking me from the house? No, that's not going to happen. You'll see. I have complete control over them, and once I'm out of here—you must let me out of here to do this. They will do what I tell them when I tell them to do it. I swear to you."

"No." She hated that word, and when he turned his back on her, she did the most incredibly stupid thing she'd ever done: she jerked him around so that he was facing her. "You dare to touch me?" His voice roared through her head and around the room like a rotunda she'd been in once.

She felt the slight breath of air. Her anger making its way out of her body felt good. It was pure, like a summer day with all the flowers in full bloom. Closing her eyes, dragging in as much as she could, LouCinda knew that she'd won this battle and that the idiot in front of her would never touch her again.

~*~

Sunny didn't mind the sunshine shining on her face. It was a habit, sitting out in the afternoon sun, she thought she could get used to. Even the slight breeze was a nice change from being inside of a restaurant all morning, too. Opening her eyes when she heard a slight sound, she closed them again when she realized who had come to visit her.

"You wished to speak to me, Sunny? I thought that the family would be out getting things ready for the funerals. They're tomorrow, correct?" Sunny explained to Lily that they were indeed tomorrow, but the food was being catered, and she was just relaxing for a bit. "I heard about what happened to William after his daughter was killed. How did he think that he could win against the shadow is beyond me. But perhaps he knew that he'd not win, and that was how he decided to end his own life. By—"

"I remember you now." Lily didn't say anything when Sunny spoke. Nodding once, she continued with her memories. "It was you, wasn't it? The day that we looked for the jar that you told me you lost. Actually, I thought that you called it your jar, but since I was only a child, four or so at the time, I misheard you. I was helping you look but not for the shard you were looking for but an actual jar."

"It's been gone to me all these years later. Your memories of it should have faded as well." Sunny told her that they had faded to almost no memory at all until recently. "What have you done to bring the memories back, Child? Surely, they didn't come to you again after all this time. Something trigger it?"

"Yes." She waited to see if Lily would ask her. When she didn't, Sunny smiled. "I found myself there yesterday. In the deep woods, sitting next to a tree without any identifying marks on it, thinking about all the deaths that LouCinda and her father caused over their lifetimes. The same tree that you were next to when my memories started to fade out that day."

"It was all I could do to keep you safe. However, losing a small piece of the crystal made it so that I could never go there and retrieve you so that you'd know who I was and why I had to do what I did. No matter how badly I wished it." Lily looked at her then, like something had only just occurred to her. "You said you found yourself there again yesterday. How did you know where to go?"

"I didn't. As I said, I was just walking around thinking. You only meant for me to stay there until such time I was old enough to realize what my role was. You meant for me to be safe, but something else happened that day that broke one of the blue crystals on your crown, and all was, as you thought, lost to you. Which in turn meant that I was as well. Correct, mother?" Lily said nothing but sat up straighter in her chair. "I've spoken to Grandma. She will forever be that to me, no matter what circumstances brought us together. I think she was glad for her role in my life for you."

"She loved you. Still does. I do as…what do you think you know, Sunshine? Tell me so that I can try and calm my heart and mind." Instead of answering her, she put out her hand and held it there. "You've found it. Haven't you? After all these years, you've finally found the piece that was missing."

"I did. It's yours now." The small piece of a crystal, no bigger than a sewing needle in width and smaller than the steel notion by half, dropped into her hand. "I was wandering around when it occurred to me that the shard had to still be there. And that it would have to be found by someone who would notice its worth. Not in monetary worth but worth more than that."

"I was holding you. You were just a child then, and I held you to me once more so that Antebellum would take you away and raise you as her own for a time. But I tripped and fell into a stone wall, and my crown, the blue stone for memory, was chipped. I found all but this piece to put it back together." The crown appeared out of nowhere, and Lily laid it across her lap. Taking the tiniest piece of matter into her hand, as if it knew what its importance was, floated down to the heart-shaped stone and slid into the smallest of crevices to complete it.

Sunny felt it fill her mind. The memories of before and since the stone had been shaped. Things that she'd missed living among the humans that her mother had dealt with and the things that would hold her future. It was gentle in its giving her the information and she was nearly asleep when it finished. The power of the completed stone filled her mind, body, and soul. Making her whole for the first time in longer than she could remember.

"I couldn't protect you after that. Not from LouCinda or her father. Not on my own, anyway. But Antebellum could and did for me, keeping me informed of your life daily. It was important that you were saved for Nash. The two of you, there were such plans for the two of you, and I worried daily because I'd been clumsy and—"

"LouCinda tried to kill you that day. You didn't trip. You were knocked away from holding me as LouCinda wanted you to fail. I don't know that she knew what was in the future for myself and her son, but she wanted me dead, and that was all she could think about at the time. My connection to magic and to you, it was the only thing that saved the two of us." Lily — Mother nodded but looked away. Sunny could feel her grief. "I've spoken to Nash. However, there wasn't a great deal that I understood at the time. Now that you've completed the gem, I know so much more than I did before. About not just his mother but also you and what your plans were in doing what you did."

"I only meant to keep you safe." Sunny told her that she had. "Yes, at the cost of missing all of your life. I should have kept you at the castle. Where I could watch you grow and become the woman that you are."

"I wouldn't be the one that I am now had you done that. The plan had been right. Put me in a place where I could learn about the humans and make a plan so that they could help with the lands and waterways. Had I been at the castle, there wouldn't have been any new information, not like we have now. I missed you, too, but we have the rest of our lives together now, and we will be able to have the best memories together going forward." She asked her about Nash. "What about him? He's going to be there as well. Right?"

"I should hope so." They both laughed. "He's

a good man. One that I had hoped would make you happy. He seems to have been able to do that."

"I love him. So very much." Mother nodded and told her that it showed on her face and in her eyes. "Thank you. He's made me very happy, and I know that he will continue to do so. However, he wants to make you happy as well. You should go and talk to him. He and his brothers are hanging out at the big house. I think they've decided to have it torn down rather than remodeled. There aren't all that many memories there for the six of them, and I think that starting fresh will give them all a better outlook on life."

"I can help them with that. You and Nash, too." She asked her mother what she meant. "You'll see. I don't have all this magic at my disposal just to make the earth clean and pretty. I can make a house green and full of good ideas as well. Yours and Nash's home will be efficient and well-maintained. Just as it should be."

"I'm sure you have much more important things to do than to help build us a house? Besides, do you even know what a hammer is?" She tsked at her. "Well, I think it's a good question. Also, what would you do differently than what we're planning now for our home?"

"Everything." The ground beneath her feet rumbled, and she had to hold on for a second before looking at her mom. "It's done."

It scared her somewhat, those two little words. It's done would imply that she had taken it upon herself to build the house the way that she had wanted it. Not that it mattered. She and Nash both were sick of living in the little house stuffed full of boxes that they couldn't open and set out yet. This might be the best thing ever for all of them. At least, she hoped so.

Chapter 8

Nash loved the house. So did his brothers, apparently, as he couldn't seem to get them to leave his home. Laughing when Sunny came into the kitchen with them, he wasn't the least bit surprised when she told them that after dinner was over, they were leaving. They had shit to do.

"You're such a spoiled sport. Did I tell you how much I love this kitchen?" Beau had just started classes to become a cook. Not a big time chef or anything like that. But he wanted to be able to make himself and, hopefully, someday, his mate a good meal that didn't take them away from their home nightly. "I didn't know that most of this stuff existed. Much less how to use it. Will you give me lessons when you get it figured out?"

"Sure. The next time I make a huge assed meal

that has seven courses, I'll do that." She smacked his brother upside the head. "Don't be a moron. I don't know how to cook. Just get the manuals on the shit and read them. That's the only way I'm going to— not that I plan on being domesticated or anything like that, but there are books on all this stuff in here somewhere. If you want to be really blown away, you should go out and have a look at the greenhouse. There are herbs and things in there that I've never heard of." He didn't bother thanking her but left to do just what she had suggested.

Nash reached for Sunny to pull her into her lap when she looked stressed. Nash decided he'd distract her enough that she could relax and let him know what was going on. It couldn't no way be about his brother wanting to learn how to cook.

"Our food is going to be delivered soon. I don't know when it happened, but there is a large dining room table in the room down the hall. Also, I forgot to mention that there wasn't a dining room when I was down there. It just appeared like it knew we were going to need a room to accommodate all of us when they came over for dinner." She asked him if he thought that the house would change to their needs. "Sounds about right, I guess. It's as good a reason as

I could think of. By the way, we have staff too. I don't know who they are as yet, but they keep appearing around the house, and I'm trying my best to ignore them when they're suddenly there. I do know that Lily said that the house was magical, so I'm going to let things go as they are until it becomes too much for me. Not there yet, but soon, I'm thinking. How are you doing today?"

"I saw one of the help. I guess they'd be called upstairs when I went to find out if we had a bedroom or not. We do, so you know. There are nine bedrooms in this place, and all of them have been furnished since I walked into them. That fucking freaked me out a little. Bedroom furniture just suddenly appeared. It's nice, don't get me wrong. It's all the things that we picked up when we went furniture shopping. But it's been set up and is ready for guests." He told her that he'd been in the living room thinking about how a fireplace would be nice, and then they had one. "Yeah, I've decided not to think about shit while I'm hanging around in this place. Also, before I forget, the things that we bought to fill out the house are already out in the rooms. The little birds that are blown glass are sitting on the window sill, just waiting for the sun to shine through them, too. If you ask me, it looks like we picked the things out with this house in mind, but I'm not going to think too heavily on that either right now."

When the doorbell rang, he didn't bother getting up to see who it might have been. More than likely, it was the food, but he had been told several times since his brothers started arriving that he had staff now and needed to allow them to do their job. He heard the voices of his brothers as they entered the large dining room to set things up.

"Do you think that if we were to just sit in here, that they'd eat their fill then leave? I've had about enough of them all being here." He laughed and told her his opinion on them leaving. "Yeah, I'm thinking that you're right. They'd just come looking for us and annoy the shit out of us more." She stood up off his lap and looked down at him. "The sooner we get them fed, the sooner they'll all go home. I don't know about you, but I think that I could sleep for a couple of years and not think a thing about it."

He had to agree. The stress of the last few days was weighing heavy on his mind and sometimes his heart, too. He'd not been a big fan of his mother or grandfather, but they were both dead now, and he couldn't help but feel their loss.

Grandfather had attacked Josiha when mother fell to the floor. Her head, removed by their leader for daring to detain him, had rolled across the floor and right at the feet of her father. He stood there for several seconds; it seemed so much longer, but that was all until he looked around the room at them all.

"Don't you even care? Look what he's done." It was then that he leapt, as his cat at the other man, and it took the six of them, as their cats, too, to remove him from their leader and calm their grandfather down. However, within seconds of them releasing him, Grandfather snarled again and then leapt at his throat. It was iffy there for a bit on whether or not he was going to kill all of them in the process. As it was, both he and Archie had been cut up, but it was Beau who had gotten a few broken ribs.

Dinner was a fun affair. Dinners with their mother had always been social but not very noisy. No conversation was started unless Mother had approved. She'd actually call them the day before dinner to give them a topic of interest to study up on so that if there was time, we'd have something intelligent to talk about. Tonight's dinner was mostly about the upcoming houses they were building. The food they were sharing and what plans they all had over the next few weeks, waiting for things to be settled up with the estates of their father and grandmother. Insurance claims had to be reworked due to them being murdered and not dying of natural causes, as their first death certificate had stated would take a few days more.

"I've gotten with an estate attorney, and he's working on gathering things up for you guys. I swear, had I known what this was going to entail, I would have just given you the shit long ago." They had a good laugh about that. Archie was never one just to hand something over to someone. He would want whatever it was fixed up so that you'd not have to mess with it nearly as much as he did. He was a good man about that sort of stuff. And he couldn't have loved him more about it. "Anyway, all the property is put into each of your names. It's being divided up equally between the six of us, and I've already made sure that you can add your mate's name to the deed as soon as you wish. Nash, as per your request, yours already has Sunny's on it."

"Thank you for that." There were other things, too, that had been divided up, and most of them had a monetary value on them that they'd not have anticipated. Rental properties that Dad had put into their names. Jewelry that he'd put in safety deposit boxes for each of them that held a great deal of gems and other items that had been in his family. None of which, come to find out, had ever been worn by their mother. "I saw the house coming down this morning. It surprised me at how quickly it came down. I don't know why, but I figured that it would take weeks for there to look like nothing had ever been there. Are you going to build on the same place?"

"No. I'm not going to build anywhere near where the house was. There is a spot that is more off the road that I've fallen in love with. I've spoken to Lily, and she said that she'd have a start on it soon for me. There are large trees surrounding it. A little pond back there. She said that when she's finished, it will look as if the house had been put there, and then the forest grew up around it. That's what I wanted." Archie exchanged a look with Sunny before he continued. "I know that we've all decided that we don't want to be up each other's asses all the time, but it's really good to know that we can just walk to each other's homes when we need to. To be honest with you, I like my solitude very much. But just knowing that each of you is so close to me that I could walk over is more appealing than I ever thought it would be."

"I agree." They hugged then, something that he was only just realizing that they do a great deal of now. He was closer to them, too, than he'd been even six months ago. He was far better off having them in his life than he'd been before, too. They were no longer his enemy. They weren't pitted against each other either. That, he thought, was worth every second of the feelings that he had against his mother for what she'd done to them all.

Nash hated his mother. Maybe that was a little harsh, he thought to himself, but he was sure that he had never loved her. It took him until this morning to come to terms with the fact that he didn't much care for his father either. He should have done more for them when he'd been alive, he'd told Sunny, rather than waiting until he was gone to make their lives better.

"I would have loved to have been able to spend time with him, learning more about becoming what he wanted us to become. Grandmother too. I don't hate her; she was as beaten as we were, but father should have done something about mother so that we could have a reasonably better life than we had." Sunny hadn't said anything, and that had nearly caused them to have a fight. But he had come to realize that she'd been right in not saying anything almost the moment his temper flared a bit. "You're thinking that because of what he did, it made us better men, right? Or some bullshit like that."

"No. I don't think that at all. Apparently, you're out to pick a fight with me, and I'm not in the mood." He watched her face as she glared at him. "Do you think it made you a better man? I have no way of knowing. You were a prick when I met you. And so you're aware, I don't like this part of you either. Picking a fight with me isn't going to bring him back. Let me ask you something, Nashville. Do you think your father would have liked being murdered? Or do you think he might well have wanted to be around now so that he could hold your children? Get to know your mates? Those are the questions you should be asking yourself. Instead of going on about how he had slighted you in some way, you should be thinking about how he's missing out on shit too."

She'd left him there. Stewing, Beau called it. And because he'd sat down with him in the kitchen after Sunny had left him, he got an earful of about how Sunny didn't understand. That had not only earned him a snort from his little brother but also a good fight in the yard when he decided that he was just too stupid to know what the adults were talking about. Nash rubbed his shoulder, where he was still sore from Beau showing him what a full-grown cat could do to someone who was stupider than he was.

After dinner was cleaned up, Sunny had shoved them out of the house. She said that she needed no drama and that they needed a good long run. He couldn't remember the last time that the six of them had gone to the woods to run, and as soon as he shifted to his other half, he could feel a freedom that he'd not been allowed in years. It felt wonderful to be able to run and play with the others where there was no malice, anger, or even the need to draw blood.

~*~

Archie sat in the lobby, waiting his turn to see his attorney. He'd been told that the person he was meeting was running late and asked to wait for her. Archie hadn't minded. After the last few days of what felt like him getting his shit together, he was easier to relax and not be short-tempered anymore. Especially since the chair he was sitting in seemed to be about the most comfy that he'd ever been in.

"Hey, mister." Archie hadn't realized he'd fallen

asleep until someone poked him. The whispered voice by his shoulder told him not to move. To go on pretending to be asleep. "There is a man in the office over there that has a gun. He's powerful pissed off at the woman in there. All I've been able to hear was that he just wants a loan."

He could hear more than the person behind him did, so he sat up in his seat and watched. He could see the gun that he was waving all over the place but not the person on the other side of the room. The young man who was wanting a loan looked to be in his mid-twenties and desperate. Standing up, Archie slowly made his way to the office.

"What is it you think you're doing?" He grinned at Sunny when she spoke to him through their link. *"Just sit your ass down and leave well enough alone. Nothing you can do there will help the situation."*

"Has he killed anyone yet?" Sunny told him that he'd not. That he was in debt to his eyeballs and would be losing his house by the end of the afternoon. *"What sort of loan does he want? Is he remodeling his home? Buying a pool with the money? What are his plans to use —"*

"He's behind in his house payments by four months. He's been working hard, but the person that he is currently

working for isn't paying on time. Wait, that's not right." When she paused talking to him, Archie stood outside the door and listened in. *"All right. It's bad. The people that he works for will pay him, he deposits the check, and then they take the money out as soon as he takes a bit of it out. Then, because they are doing that, everything that he has paid is now subject to bounced check charges. And you know how that works, I'm sure. You start an avalanche of check-bouncing charges that seem to never end. He just wants to get his account set up so that it stops happening to him. In addition to him living in the house with his wife and three kids, he's also trying to support his parents and his wife's younger brother. He's a good man, by all accounts. So how are we going to help him?"*

"How are we going to help him? You told me to sit down and let it go." He told Sunny to make sure that the police don't bother them while he figures something out. *"I don't know what I'll do, but I have to do something."*

"I can do that." After clearing his throat and having the younger man turn to him, Archie smiled at the man. *"You probably don't care about his name right now, but it's David Goss."*

"My name is Archie. I could hear that you're having problems, and I'd like to help you out." The man told him his name and that he was working with the attorney. "Yeah, that doesn't look like it's getting you very far. How about you and I sit down here after you put the gun away and have a conversation? I really do want to help you."

"No one wants to help me. I don't even know why I thought that this might work." David looked at the woman and then back at him. "I fucked up here. I'm only just realizing that no one is going to help me for sure now that I've dragged a gun into this." He put out the gun toward him, and Archie took it. "You can have this. It's not loaded, anyway. I just…Christ, my wife is going to kill me."

An hour after meeting the younger man, Archie felt like he was on top of the world. Not only did he hire an attorney from the offices that he was in to represent David, but he also was able to help him file a lawsuit against the company that he'd been working for. The Attorney, Mrs. Vander Welk, it had been her office that he'd been directed to, was helping them file paperwork so that the bank couldn't take their home, car, or no utilities shut off. Taking them out to lunch and inviting his wife to join them, David was working for him now as a foreman while the construction was going on around his home. After that was finished, he promised him he'd have work lined up to keep him working all the time. Archie even made arrangements for a large line of credit to be put at the stores around town so that not only could David feed his family but also to make sure that they had clothing and diapers when they needed them as well.

"You're a good man, Mr. Sheppard. I can't thank you enough for this." Archie said that he had enjoyed it, too. It was good helping someone. "You did me a solid, and as soon as I can, I'll pay this all back to you. I swear."

"You just pay it forward. I hear that a great deal, but at this moment, I think that it really means something to me. As soon as you find yourself up on your feet, David, you pay it forward, help someone else that is on the verge." David and his wife both said that they would. "Good. Now, we have this all worked out, and if you show up at this address tomorrow to go over the things that Mrs. Vander Welk needs to sue your company, you should be able to take a deep breath from now on."

On his way home, he stopped off to get something to eat. Archie hadn't felt this useful in a very long time and was going to treat himself to not just one of his favorite meals, but he decided that he was going to eat in the restaurant rather than take it home. As soon as he ordered, he got up to go to the salad bar.

Archie, being a cat, wasn't always keen on green veggies. But today, with all that had been going on too in the past few weeks, he knew that he had to start taking better care of himself and his cat. Besides, this particular salad bar had all kinds of protein things, like boiled eggs as well as ham and turkey, so he could really load up his lettuce. When he sat down to enjoy it, he realized that he had more meat and cheeses than he did lettuce. It was all good, he told himself. It was still a nice salad.

When he had gone to the salad bar twice more, he came back to his table to find Nash sitting at his table. Not bothering with asking him what he wanted, he watched as he got up and made himself a huge meat-only salad, too. As soon as the waitress brought him his pizza, Nash took two slices for himself and rolled them into a long tube, eating them nearly in one bite.

"You're paying for dinner. I hope you know that." Nash nodded. "Why are you bothering me here? I was having a good day until you showed up.

Where is Sunny? I have a feeling she'd not be too thrilled about taking my meal. She likes me."

"Yeah? Well, she loves me, and I get to have sex with her. A lot of it." Rolling his eyes at his brother, he asked him what he was doing there. "I have some questions for you. I don't know that you'll have all the answers, but it's important that I voice them."

"All right. But you're still paying for my dinner." Waving him off, Archie had a feeling that he was going to leave him with the bill. Not that he really minded, but it was the principle of the thing. "What did you want to know?"

"First, and this shouldn't be a surprise to you, Josiha stepped down from his position just about an hour ago. He is going to hang out at the offices for our shadow until you take over. I hadn't any idea that it was a done deal for you to be taking over." He said that he'd not known that either. "You should go by there soon and have a talk with him. Sunny said to tell you not to go alone, either. For you to take me."

"I can do that. What else?" He told him the second part as the waitress came to the table. After ordering another pizza for them, he had to think why it was important that Nash thought it was imperative that he took the job. "Who cares who runs the shadow? I mean, I guess I could do it. However, I'd be a bit more present than Joshia ever was. Not to say that I'm taking it, but he's been lax for a long time."

"He has. I talked with Lily this morning. Did you know that if you take over the shadow, you become an immortal? Lily seems to think that he's been at it for so long. He was just doing his time. Bored, she thought that he had seen too much and was bored out of his mind with the shit, so just ignored it." Archie could see that, too. It was why he decided that he was going to go to college and try something else. Anything else that would stimulate his mind and body. "Also, Lily said that as soon as you take it, she seems to think that it's a foregone conclusion that you will take it, you'll get a shit ton of power. I don't know what that might entail, but she told me that you need to be with people in the event that it puts you down for a while."

"Good to know. Though again, I don't know that I'd take the job." Nash nodded but didn't comment. "What else? You said several things."

"When Lily acknowledges that Sunny is her daughter, we'll get a lot of power, a great deal of it. I was told that the family will get some as well. While I have an idea that it will make us powerful, I don't have a lot of details about what that might mean for us." Nodding again, he ate the last slice of his pizza. The second one was coming toward them even as he realized that he was still really hungry. "Also, and this one boggles my mind to no end. We'll have an endless supply of funds. I had to ask because — well, endless? What the hell does that even mean? Anyway, we'll get that as soon as she does her thing."

"Endless, huh? Well, I guess it would be nice to be able to help out the shadow. I know it's not all that big of one. I think that Joshia said that it was less than fifty cats. With us included." Nash told him that there was a great deal of money already in the coffers for the shadow that hadn't been touched in decades. "What the fuck? Do you mean that there could have been all these improvements, and he just sat on it, not doing a thing? Christ, no wonder there are only fifty people in the shadow. No one is getting help so they just went to greener pastures. Anything else I need to be made aware of?"

"Yes, plenty." When he didn't say anything more, Archie looked at his brother. He seemed to be lost in thought, and he found himself reaching beyond where they were to see if he could figure anything out. "Archie, do you trust me?"

"With all that I am. What's going on?" He leaned toward him, which surprised him that he was speaking rather than using their link if he wanted it to be a secret. "Nash, you're scaring me a little."

"The three people over there at the booth just to the right of the front counter are planning to rob the place. The manager knows about it, she's in over her head with owing them a great deal of money from her brother's debt." Archie asked if they were planning to hurt anyone. "Yes. All of us. I need you to take my hand, Archie. Just for a second so that I can protect us both."

He didn't hesitate at all but put his hand out so that Nash could do whatever was necessary to keep them safe. The brush of his hand over his was warm, but he could feel whatever he gave him start to heat up his hand, then up and over his body.

"Don't pass out on me." Shaking his head, Archie said that he was a little dizzy. "Dizzy is better than dead. Just follow my lead, and we'll get everyone out of here in one piece. All right?"

"Yes. Do whatever you need." When Nash stood up, so did Archie. He wasn't as dizzy as he'd been at first, but his body was beginning to hum with whatever Nash had done to him. When Nash headed for the three people in the corner, he told him to go to the back room and help the manager. He was nearly back there when he heard the sound of one pissed-off cat and then nothing at all.

"You can't be back here." Archie told the man making pizzas that the place was about to be robbed and that he needed for him to get out. "All right. I'm done here. This is the fourth time this place has been hit in a year. I'm not coming back."

The man tossed his apron onto the half-finished pizza he'd been making and left by the back door. Alarms were still going off when Archie entered the office of the manager. The woman was sitting there with a gun to her mouth. Sitting down, she stared at him with her eyes full of falling tears. She pulled the gun out of her mouth long enough to tell him to go away.

"I can't do that, I'm afraid. Please don't do whatever you're thinking of doing." She said that she didn't want to go to prison for someone else's trouble. "No, I can see that. Where is your brother while you're dealing with this shit here?"

"Dead. He decided to get himself killed and

leave me hanging. Wait, how did you know I had a brother? Who's been talking to you?" Archie told her that he had read her mind. Then he asked her why she thought that killing herself was going to help. "Great. A loony reading my mind. And it won't solve anything, but I won't have to deal with it either. I'm sick of being everyone — you know, I'm not even supposed to be managing this place. I'm just a waitress who started helping out the real manager when she was too drunk to care what happened here on a daily basis. Since I like to have a check and food in my belly, I took over."

"That's commendable of you. Brave too. Where is the manager right now?" She told him she didn't know, but he came in to take the deposits to the bank at night. "No doubt after you're closed. Are you sure that the money is getting to the bank?"

"No. And again, I don't care all that much. I have the money witnessed by an off duty cop before I leave. He records it all for me, and then I email it to corporate and to both him and myself. I might be a waitress, but I know how to cover my ass when I need to." He grinned at her, and she cocked a brow at him. "I don't know what you think might be funny, mister, but I have shit going on, and you're not helping me get to the end."

"My brother, you've not met him as yet, but he's taken care of the problem in the lobby for you. I don't know what he did—I know that I would have killed them, but then Nash has a better head on his shoulders than I do most of the time." She asked him to get out of her office. "Sure. But in the meantime, do you want to have dinner with me tonight?"

"No. Now leave me." He did leave her, but he wasn't sure that he'd be staying away. She was a spitfire, and he wanted to get to know her. Before he was to the dining area again, it hit him like a ton of bricks. He'd just met his mate. Turning to go back and talk to her more, he heard the sound of a gunshot before he reached her office.

"Christ."

AWARD WINNING, BESTSELLING AUTHOR

Kathi Barton, a winner of the Pinnacle Book Achievement Award and a best-selling author on Amazon and All Romance books, lives in Nashport, Ohio, with her husband, Paul. When not creating new worlds and romance, Kathi and her husband enjoy camping and going to auctions. She can also be seen at county fairs with her husband, an artist and potter.

Her muse, a cross between Jimmy Stewart and Hugh Jackman, brings her stories to life for her readers in a way that has them coming back time and again for more. Her favorite genre is paranormal romance, with a great deal of spice. You can visit Kathi online and drop her an email if you'd like. She loves hearing from her fans. aaronskiss@gmail.com.

www.ingramcontent.com/pod-product-compliance
Lightning Source LLC
Chambersburg PA
CBHW020752210626
46807CB00018B/2689